★

A HEAVY SICK FEELING SETTLED IN HER STOMACH

She didn't want to look.

She got up and pushed through the tangled salmonberry to the creek, waded across, and climbed up the other side. The cap was lying a few yards from the bank. She got close enough to see the words written across the front. Holiday Acres. Everyone who worked there wore one. She forced herself to examine the area. Scraps of cloth lay scattered over the ground, their red plaid almost lost in the mud. Extending from one of the scraps was a hand. Two of the fingers were missing.

She lurched back to the creek and knelt there until her stomach stopped heaving. She filled her hard hat with water, splashed some on her face, rinsed her mouth out, then rummaged through her pockets for a roll of flagging. Without a backward glance she tore a piece off, tied it to one of the cedars, crossed the creek, and took off up the hill, leaving a trail of yellow ribbon.

★

COLD TRACKS

LEE WALLINGFORD

WORLDWIDE®

TORONTO • NEW YORK • LONDON
AMSTERDAM • PARIS • SYDNEY • HAMBURG
STOCKHOLM • ATHENS • TOKYO • MILAN
MADRID • WARSAW • BUDAPEST • AUCKLAND

COLD TRACKS

A Worldwide Mystery/February 1993

Published by arrangement with Walker and Company.

ISBN 0-373-26114-4

Printed in U.S.A.

To Kate Wilhelm and Damon Knight,
with thanks to Jim Damitio

PROLOGUE

FRANK CARVER drove slowly down the central Oregon coast. It was August. The highway was clogged with motor homes, but he didn't mind. He had not had time like this for years—time to take the scenic route, mosey through the little towns, stop to walk on the beach. It felt like a vacation, except that vacations had always included his wife and daughters. They were gone now, the two girls married, his wife—former wife—busy selling real estate. And this was not a vacation. It was a permanent, final end to twenty years with the Seattle police.

Not retirement, though that was something he had considered. But he was only fifty-three, nowhere near ready to buy a cabin on a lake and rust away into oblivion. Retirement was not what he needed. Frank searched for the right word as the bays and headlands slipped past his window on one side, the dark, fir-covered hills on the other. That was a luxury in itself, time to search for the right word. All those years of reports, dashed off when he was tired, rushed, when he didn't have time to care. Well, he had time now. Not retirement. Retreat, perhaps, or refuge—in a way he was a refugee, retreating from the grim reality of police work in a big city. His new job—law enforcement officer for the Neskanie National Forest—was supposed to be police work, too, but he had smiled when he read the job description. Fire investigations? Timber theft? It sounded like a holiday.

The coast highway climbed another headland. Frank pulled into a wayside stop and got out. The breeze, cold in spite of the sunshine, tugged briskly at his shirt. He leaned against the low rock surrounding the viewpoint area. Directly below, cliffs dropped three hundred feet to the ocean. Hardy grasses and succulents clung to the shelves of weathered rock. Waves pounded dully against the foot of the cliffs. Frank looked along the coastline, picking out a river, a bridge, a small town at the edge of a bay. Behind the town rose ranks of dark, folded hills, marching inland.

The highway twisted down the back side of the headland, crossing ravines and small streams. Frank came out on the flat and reached the bridge, a span of arches flung across the river like a bird in flight. WPA work, he guessed. The Neskanie River slipped away below, wide and slow here, where it reached the ocean. He stopped for lunch in the town, then strolled along the bay front, past the marina and docks. Fishing boats jostled one another in the protected waters of the bay, some clean, some dirty, all of them smelling of fish and the ocean.

On his way back to the car, he stopped at the marina to ask about the charter fishing boats. His greatest regret in leaving Seattle was leaving Puget Sound. For years he had rewarded himself at the end of a tough case with a weekend out on the water. He would rent a boat with some friends, or take his family along and fish by himself while Minnie and the girls hiked or lay in the sun. Well, he would have plenty of time for fishing now.

Back in his car, he turned east, off 101, and took the highway into the Coast Range. He eyed the Neskanie as he drove. The water was low now, after the dry summer, but the river was famed for its salmon and steelhead. Once he had decided to leave Seattle, Frank had not really cared where he went. One day, looking through some job announcements, the name Neskanie had caught his eye, bringing up images of hip boots and waders, rushing water, long, peaceful afternoons. He had never cared if he caught anything. He always came back refreshed, restored—there he was, searching for the right word again. Renewed. That was what he needed, to be renewed.

Marinas and fishing camps gave way to stands of timber. The road snaked and turned, a narrow ribbon of pavement threaded through the overhanging firs. The dense canopy blotted out the sun; brush grew up the edges of the road. Frank, accustomed to city lights and traffic, glanced uneasily at the towering trees. Occasionally the valley opened, giving glimpses of clearcuts and distant ridges.

He drove faster, suddenly anxious to reach the Neskanie Supervisor's Office before it closed. He was already calling it the SO, picking up the Forest Service jargon. As the first special agent assigned to the forest, he would be based in Longmont, in the Willamette Valley. He would be on call, though, for the Neskanie's five districts, scattered in little towns through the Coast Range. If he remembered the map correctly, he should be coming to one of them now.

Galina. The road dropped abruptly into a large, open valley. Fields and pastures lay along both sides of the river. Frank slowed down. The ranger station was a huddle of green buildings just past the mill. Then a small store, a cluster of pickup trucks in front of the tavern, the school. A few more houses straggled along the road, and then he sped up again, driving through the golden haze of late afternoon. Longmont was only thirty miles farther on.

THE FALL RAINS were late that year. The water stayed low in the rivers, and the fishing was poor. In September, while he was collecting evidence for a timber theft case, Frank got lost in the woods twice. Then a key witness took one look at him and refused to talk until the county sheriff, whom he knew, sat in on the interview. In October Frank and the same sheriff, raiding a pot plantation, stumbled upon a crude booby trap made with fishhooks. It was penny-ante stuff, and Frank found it wonderfully, refreshingly dull. There was plenty of work, but no shootings, no bodies, no murders.

ONE

THE NEWLY PAINTED farmhouse stood by itself, just where Elk Creek flowed into Tenmile River. Five miles downstream, Tenmile River joined the Neskanie on its way to the sea. In the farmhouse lived Ginny Trask, fire dispatcher for Galina Ranger District, and her nine-year-old daughter, Rebecca.

Ginny sat on the back steps with a sketchbook open on her lap, drawing bunnies. Rebecca's pet rabbit hopped lazily across the yard. It was November first, very mild, and the dandelions were still in bloom. A half dozen versions of the rabbit hopped across Ginny's page. The one she was working on right now wore a sweatshirt with a picture of Beethoven. The screen door creaked, closed quietly, and Rebecca came out to stand at her elbow.

"How are you feeling, honey?" Ginny asked, adding a final stroke to the rabbit's tail. "Any better?"

"A little bit."

Ginny looked up at her daughter. Rebecca's heart-shaped face was thin and pale beneath her fading tan. Her dark hair straggled untidily down to her shoulders, but her eyes were clear, with no sign of last night's fever—a fever that had not been helped by a stomach full of Halloween candy. Rebecca was looking at the drawing with a critical eye.

"You've made his ears too long."

"He's a special long-eared rabbit. So he can hear Beethoven better."

Rebecca sat down on the steps and squeezed her eyes shut. "I see something with my magic eye."

This was an old game with them, one they had started before Rebecca could handle a pencil. She described something she saw inside her mind, and Ginny drew a picture of it. Rebecca had been capable of drawing her own pictures for some time now, but they both still enjoyed the game. Ginny flipped her pad to a clean sheet of paper.

"Tell me, Rebecca, what you see," she intoned.

Instead, Rebecca opened her eyes. "Mom, do you think Bigfoot is real?"

Ginny looked at her in surprise. "Well, I don't know. Some people think so."

"But what about when people see one, like last summer? Do you think they really see one?"

Rebecca's eyes were serious. Like all the kids in Galina, she had been excited by the reports of a Sasquatch on the Neskanie Indian Reservation. But that had been three months ago. Why was she bringing it up again now?

"I think Laughing Charlie and his son believe they saw a Bigfoot," Ginny said carefully. "What do you think?"

"I don't know, either." Rebecca kicked at the steps, then turned her attention to the rabbit, who had come closer in hope of a handout. "Alexander," she crooned. "Want some lettuce?"

Ginny gazed at her, feeling uneasily that something was not right. Rebecca's hair parted over her bent head, revealing a couple of knobby vertebrae. Ginny fought down an urge to lean over and kiss the exposed patch of skin.

Inside the house the phone started ringing. Ginny got up with reluctance. After five years as Galina's fire dispatcher, she could sense when a phone call meant extra work.

She was right. It was Len Whittaker, her boss. "Glad I caught you at home. The SO just called. We're shipping a twenty-man crew at five o'clock."

There went the rest of Saturday afternoon. Ginny would have to round up the crew, make sure they had their gear, and arrange for transportation to Longmont. Fire control at the SO would handle everything from there.

"Is Susie around?" she asked. "Can she take Rebecca?" Susie Meissner, Len's grown stepdaughter, often baby-sat for her.

"Sure, I'll let her know. If you're coming by here, maybe I'll ride in to the station with you."

"They got you, too, huh?"

"Line boss. Oh well, I haven't been to California since last summer." Len chuckled. Galina's fire management officer loved going away on fires, which suited

Ginny just fine. She liked her job better when he was not around.

She went back to the porch and sat down beside Rebecca. "That was Len. I've got to go in to the station. Put Alexander back into his hutch and I'll drop you off at Holiday Acres."

"Aw, Mom."

"I know, honey, I'm sorry, but that's—"

"—just the way it is." Rebecca made a face and stood up.

"Bring your new library book. Maybe you can read it to Susie."

"Mom, she doesn't *like* horse stories."

"Get."

A few minutes later they were ready. Ginny piled Rebecca and her bag of books and toys into the car and pulled out onto the road. Tenmile River was low, in some places just a trickle of scummy water between stretches of bedrock. A smoky haze filled the valley. Ginny rolled the car windows up to keep out the dust. She wished it would rain.

A sign the size of a small billboard marked the driveway to Holiday Acres Christmas Tree Farm. She took the turn and let the car lug up the hill, optimistic that this time they would make it in third gear.

"There's Susie!" Rebecca cried, hugging her canvas bag.

Ginny slowed the car to keep the dust down and came to a stop. Susie was raking leaves in front of the rambling split-level that housed the Whittaker-

Meissner family and the Holiday Acres business offices. Ginny rolled down the window.

"Len said you could take Rebecca this afternoon. Is that OK?"

"Sure, it's fine." She gave them a wistful smile. Though Susie Meissner was twenty-five, Ginny always thought of her as younger, perhaps because she was shy and overweight. She was wearing jeans and a baggy sweatshirt—Ginny could not recall ever seeing her in anything else—and a couple of leaves had caught in her hair. Rebecca got out and set her bag on the grass.

"Where's Len?" Ginny asked. "I'm supposed to pick him up."

"Taking a shower. He was down by the creek all morning, trying out a backhoe."

They heard the front door open; then Len came out with Harriet, Susie's mother.

"Hey there, Ginny," Len called. "That was fast." He came striding toward the car, a weathered, lean man in his late forties. He tossed his fire pack into the backseat, kissed Harriet, and got in.

Harriet leaned over to peer through the driver's window. "Come have dinner with us, Ginny, when you get done. The Gilmores are coming over."

"Sounds great," Ginny said. "I'll try to make it."

"Danny's home, too," Harriet added. "I'll tell him you're coming." Danny Meissner was Harriet's son.

Ginny glanced up, but the older woman's face was carefully neutral. That was just like Harriet, getting her to say yes and then adding a catch. She never felt completely comfortable around Danny, and Harriet knew it.

She pushed down her annoyance and turned to Rebecca. "Listen, kiddo, you keep out of trouble."

Susie, who was quite strong in spite of her soft appearance, swung Rebecca up onto her shoulders. "We'll have a great time. We're going to make pies this afternoon, and talk about all our new books."

Ginny let the clutch out and bumped the car back down the hill. "When did Danny get back?" she asked.

"Couple of days ago," Len said, rearranging the items in his fire pack. "Back for a little vacation, he said."

"But he was here just a few weeks ago. I thought that was his vacation."

Len nodded. "Yeah. Funny kind of job, if you can take that much time off. Anyway, he's sponging off his mother again."

Poor Danny Meissner, Ginny thought as she pulled out onto the Neskanie highway. Len's stepson was a real puzzle. He had a degree in biology, and from what she heard he was a fine technician—top notch when it came to hands-on lab work. In spite of which, he had never kept a job for more than a few months. Or a girlfriend. Ginny was not looking forward to seeing him again.

The parking lot at the ranger station was deserted. Ginny unlocked the door to Dispatch and flipped the radio on while Len rounded up his equipment. Then she got busy finding twenty fire fighters available on what might be the last fine Saturday of the year.

She had located eight of them when Len stuck his head through the door. His fire pack was slung over one shoulder, and a canteen and radio dangled from his belt. The most remarkable thing about him, though, was his Nomex jumpsuit. Fireproof and brilliant yellow, it covered him from his neck and wrists to his ankles.

Ginny propped the phone on her shoulder. "See you got your fancy duds on." The phone kept ringing. Most of the crew were probably down by the river, a fishing pole in one hand and a beer in the other. She hung up. "I got a ride for you into the SO. Should be here in a few minutes."

Len gave her a preoccupied nod and leaned over her shoulder to peer at the crew list.

"Don't worry," she said. "I'll get them. Anything special I should do while you're gone?"

He straightened up to inspect the burn schedule pinned to the wall. "Yeah. Cancel the Cripple Elk burn on Monday. You'll be too shorthanded. Make sure Silviculture gets a copy of that list of unburned acres. Maybe they can talk some sense into the ranger."

A Forest Service pickup swung into the compound and passed the window. Len grabbed his fire pack. "There's my ride. See you whenever."

SHE REACHED Bear Taylor a few minutes later, then struck out with three names in a row. Nino Alvarez, who worked in Silviculture, was next on her list. He was a sure bet. How many times had he told her he was available for fires? Nino lived in the station's old bunkhouse during the week, but spent the weekends with his brothers in Harmony, fifty miles away.

"You have that phone number, yes?" he had asked in August, during his first week on the job.

"I've got it. You hungry for overtime or something?"

He had looked puzzled for a moment, then touched his red hat and grinned. "Hungry. Yes, hungry for the big paycheck."

Whenever he saw her after that, he grinned, tapped his hat, and reminded her. "Still hungry."

She dialed. "Hello. Is Nino Alvarez there?"

"Nino, no, no, *qué pasa*? Who is this?" The woman broke into a torrent of Spanish. It ended abruptly; then a man's voice came on. *"No está aquí,"* he said. "Nino is not home." He hung up.

Ginny frowned. At this rate she would be here all night. As she made the next call, the first fire fighters showed up, two college students spending their first season on the crew. They looked like old hands now, but they couldn't hide their excitement. "Ka-ching, ka-ching," they joked, ringing up imaginary overtime.

The rest of the crew drifted in, cluttering up the hall with their packs and boots, bumming pinches of Copenhagen, trading stories about California fires. Finally the crew boss herded his nineteen fire fighters, fifteen men and four women, out to the vans Ginny had lined up. They tossed their packs on top with the chain saw and piled inside. The motors revved, tires kicked up dust, and they were off.

The station felt unnaturally quiet after they were gone. Ginny kept the radio volume down, listening to the SO dispatcher chatter with the districts as she finished her paperwork. It sounded like half the people on the Neskanie were on their way to California. Well, that was fine with her. She liked a quiet week every now and then.

IT WAS PAST SIX when Ginny pulled up in front of the Holiday Acres house. She got out of her car and leaned against the fender for a moment to enjoy the view. At her house the sun went behind Jackson Ridge about four in the afternoon, so a full-scale sunset was something of a treat. The farm was quiet. Ginny found herself straining to hear voices, footsteps, any sounds of human activity. She jumped as a chicken cackled loudly from the henhouse across the driveway. Who was she kidding, anyhow? She was nervous about seeing Danny. The western clouds were still ablaze when she went up to the front door and knocked.

To her relief, it was Harriet who answered. Ginny followed her through the living room, her stomach tightening again. In just a minute she would see him. Voices—Susie's and Rebecca's—came from the kitchen. Ginny stalled by stopping to poke her head through the doorway and say hello.

The kitchen smelled of chicken and apple pie. Rebecca looked up from the vegetables she was cutting. "Hi, Mom. We're making a salad."

"Get the crew off?" Susie asked. "Fifteen minutes to dinner."

Ginny caught up with Harriet. "I sure appreciate Susie taking Rebecca on such short notice," she said as they stepped out onto the redwood deck behind the house. No one was there.

Harriet waved her to a chair and sat down herself, pursing her lips. She was a sturdy woman in her late forties, with salt-and-pepper hair and sharp blue eyes. She and Len Whittaker had been married for less than a year. "Does her good," Harriet said. "Susie, I mean. Keeps her mind off her problems."

Ginny looked up. "Oh-oh. Is Susie having problems again?"

"No more than usual. I just wish she'd get off her fanny and *do* something for a change, instead of reading those damn romances."

"Well, she conned Rebecca into fixing dinner," Ginny said. "That must have taken some doing." Harriet had never given her daughter much credit for running the house, even though she had been doing it since leaving high school.

"Ah, here comes Danny," Harriet said. Her face softened into a smile as she watched the tall, thin figure emerge from a stand of firs and come up the road.

Ginny's stomach fluttered, then settled into place as Danny Meissner came across the lawn. His sand-colored hair was longer than she remembered, his blue eyes bright against a new tan, but he had the same slightly displaced air as always. He looked up, saw Ginny, and quickly looked away.

When he reached the deck, however, he was smiling. "Hey, Ginny. How's the radio queen?" He pulled a chair closer, sat down, and gave her knee a friendly squeeze. "Hear you shipped the old man off to California."

Ginny smiled in spite of herself. Danny was easy to like when he was in one of his irreverent moods, but she still wished he would not touch her.

Harriet sighed loudly. "I don't think Len's been home more than three weeks in a row since we got married."

"You'll see plenty of him this winter," Ginny said, "once fire season's over." Danny's hand was still resting on her knee. She moved it to his own leg.

"Well," said Harriet complacently, "at least Danny's back for a while."

Danny grinned. "Back to the old nest."

"How's California?" Ginny asked politely.

"Beautiful. Great place to visit."

"Dale and I went to San Francisco once," Ginny said. "Kind of a second honeymoon."

Their discussion of San Francisco's tourist attractions was interrupted by the arrival of the Gilmores. Joe Gilmore was a retired logger. Magda had worked at Holiday Acres for years, running the packing crew in the fall and shearing trees in the summer. She was from Poland—a child refugee after the war—and still spoke with a faint accent. The Gilmores, who had a married daughter in the Bay Area, joined the conversation.

A few minutes later the cook's triangle sounded behind them. Rebecca stood just outside the kitchen door, banging away with a big metal spoon. When Danny stood up she caught sight of him and stopped the racket.

"Danny!" she cried. She dashed across the deck and threw herself against him. "Susie said you were back. Where've you been all day? I've got a million things to tell you."

Danny unwrapped her arms from his waist. "What's your mother been feeding you, anyhow? You've grown at least three inches. Here, I've brought you something." He fished around in his shirt pocket and pulled out a small, narrow package.

"What is it?" Rebecca pulled the paper off, then opened the box. Inside was a silver tube, about the size of a fat pencil. "What is it?" she asked again, turning it over in her hand.

"A magnifying glass. For field work. See, here's the lens." Danny knelt down to show her.

Rebecca had always liked Danny. He had known her since she was born, when he was not much more than a kid himself. He'd gone on picnics with her, taken her horseback riding, fishing, mushroom hunting. Ginny's reservations about him took a backseat whenever she saw him with her daughter.

Finally they all went into the dining room. Susie dished out chicken from the electric skillet while Danny played host, pouring wine for everyone. Biscuits steamed under a checkered towel in the center of the table. Rebecca slipped into a chair between Susie and Danny. She loved dinner at Holiday Acres, and Ginny knew why—there was so much of everything, especially dessert. Susie usually gave her a glass of wine, too—half wine and half water, but in a real wineglass.

Susie finished serving everyone and started to eat. Perspiration glistened on her forehead, and one cheek was smeared with flour. Seen side by side, she and Danny were clearly siblings. They had their father's sandy hair and their mother's blue eyes, and they both ate quickly, with their heads bent over their plates. Danny caught Ginny's glance and gave her a quick, almost sheepish smile.

Ginny kept her eye on Rebecca while they ate. Even though she had been sick yesterday, she had insisted on wearing her princess costume to the Halloween party at the grade school. There had been a lot of good costumes—two boys had even come as Bigfoot, and Ginny wondered now if that had been behind Rebecca's question earlier in the afternoon.

Rebecca did not look good. Not sick, exactly, more—ruffled. As though something was happening inside and had not quite made it to the surface. Last night she had been feverish, complaining that her stomach hurt. Twice Ginny had heard her get up and walk around the room. The second time she had gone in and found Rebecca standing at the opened window, her eyes looking scared in the light from the full moon. Ginny had helped her back into bed, and she had immediately fallen asleep.

Magda was talking now, asking Danny about his job.

"I don't really have a job right now," Danny said. "The project I was working on came to an end."

There was an uncomfortable silence. Susie's wineglass clattered against her plate as she set it down, spilling a few drops on the tablecloth.

"You're back for good, then?" Magda asked.

"As long as the old lady will have me."

Ginny glanced at Harriet, who seemed to have no qualms about her older child moving back in. She wondered how Len felt about having Danny under the same roof again.

"Actually," said Danny, helping himself to another piece of chicken, "I'm hoping to work on a little project of my own while I'm here."

"And what is that?" Magda asked.

"Sasquatch," Danny said. "Bigfoot. I hear one's been seen around here."

The silence this time had a stunned quality. Joe was the first to break it, speaking with more enthusiasm than he had shown all evening. "You'll be talking to Laughing Charlie, then. Quite a few of the boys went up there, you know."

The Bigfoot sighting that summer had stirred up the whole town. The local rifle club—Joe was the president—had rented the fire hall to show a video that included the famous 1967 footage from northern California. A number of people had gone out with guns, to the dismay of the Forest Service, which had already closed the tinder-dry woods to loggers. A few questionable footprints had been found on Jackson Ridge, and then the furor had died down.

"There's been lots of sightings around Galina," said Danny.

"Not many since the fifties, though," Joe replied. "Why, your own grandpa—"

"Don't start," said Harriet in a weary voice.

"Aw, come on, Harriet, the boy's heard the story before."

"So have I, about a million times."

"I haven't," Rebecca piped up.

Ginny tried to silence her with a meaningful glance, but the damage was done. Joe shifted in his seat so that he could see Rebecca clearly. "Why, Harriet's own papa, Billy Lundgren, saw a Bigfoot back when he was just a boy. Not too far from here, either. See," Joe said, getting comfortable, "Billy was the whistle punk on his dad's summer show—"

"What's a whistle punk?" Rebecca demanded.

There was an audible sigh from Harriet, but Joe was not to be deterred. "Why, the whistle punk passes the signals on a logging show. Don't have 'em anymore, of course. Used to be a boy's first job out in the woods. Anyhow, as I was saying, Billy Lundgren was way back up Elk Creek with his daddy's operation. They'd shut down for lunch, and Billy took off to see what was on top of the ridge. He was beating through the brush when he saw it, standing next to a tree, just as casual as you please.''

He paused to gauge his audience. Rebecca, Danny, and Susie were absorbed. Harriet looked bored and a little irked. Magda looked worried, perhaps because of Harriet. Ginny was fascinated. She recalled hearing this story mentioned last summer, but had not connected it with Harriet's family.

"What did it look like?" Rebecca asked.

"Taller than a man, with huge shoulders and a small head, covered all over with short, brown hair. Kind of like a bear's coat, Billy said. Well, no sooner did Billy lay eyes on the critter than it turned around and humped itself out of there. Billy did the same.''

They had questions after that. Joe did his best to answer them, making up a few of the more colorful details, Ginny suspected, so as not to disappoint anyone.

"Now Laughing Charlie says he's seen one," Joe finished. "Well, maybe. It's been forty years since anyone made that claim. Say," he added, turning to Danny. "I've got a bunch of newspaper clippings from back then. Used to be pretty interested myself, when I was a kid.''

Magda finally succeeded in catching his eye, and Joe fell into an embarrassed silence.

"I'd like to take a look at them," Danny said. "Grandpa's sighting must have been, what, eighty years ago? But those Sasquatch are still around." He warmed to the topic. "Maybe I'll talk to some of the guys about getting up a real search. Early December would be perfect. Leaves are off the brush, visibility's better, and the ground hasn't frozen yet."

Harriet found her voice. "What on earth are you talking about?"

"Bigfoot. I'm going to look for Bigfoot."

"Not in December." Harriet looked dazed. "Not in the middle of the Christmas tree harvest."

"You can get along without me," Danny said. "You've got Len now, remember? He'll be glad to have me out of the way."

Harriet shook her head. "Danny, I can't throw money away on something like this."

"I don't need money," Danny snapped. He glared at his mother, then turned away. "Sorry, Harriet. I'll talk to you about it later."

There was another awkward silence. Susie collected plates and started pouring coffee. Rebecca wriggled in her chair, until Ginny gave her a look that meant "settle down."

"Well, anyhow, I'll get those clippings out for you," Joe Gilmore said. "Just give me a call when you want to come over."

Rebecca was almost bouncing in her chair. Ginny gave her another admonishing look.

"But I saw one!" Rebecca burst out.

"What?" Ginny stared at her daughter. "What did you see?"

"Bigfoot! That's what I saw last night."

Danny whistled under his breath.

"Where did you see it?" Ginny asked.

"From my window. I woke up, and it was so hot. I opened the window to let some air in, and then I saw it!"

"Humph," Harriet said, but Ginny was remembering Rebecca crouched beside the open window, her wide, blank eyes reflecting the moonlight.

"What did you see, exactly?" Danny asked. He and Joe were both watching Rebecca with great interest.

"It was walking past our house, up the creek. It was big, like a really big man, and its shoulders were funny. Like a hunchback."

"A hunchback!"

Rebecca nodded. "Like the man in *The Secret Garden*."

Ginny gazed thoughtfully at her daughter. Rebecca read a lot, and she was imaginative, but she was also very truthful.

"It was like a dream," Rebecca said. "Except that I was awake."

"Jesus," Danny murmured. His eyes were sparkling. "What do you say, Joe? Want to go over to their place and look for tracks tomorrow?"

"Whoa, Danny." Ginny held up a hand. "Wait a minute. One sick nine-year-old might have seen something in the dark."

"She might have seen Bigfoot, practically in our backyard. Come on, Ginny, don't start sounding like Harriet."

At the mention of her name, Harriet stood up. She fixed her son with a stony stare. "Ginny is being perfectly reasonable. If she has any sense, she'll take Rebecca home right now. The child is obviously sick."

"She was fine this afternoon," Susie said. Her voice faltered, and she turned away from her mother's withering glance.

"But I did see it," Rebecca said. "I really did."

Ginny pushed her chair out. "Come on, Rebecca. It's time we were getting along, anyway."

They gathered their things. Ginny thanked Susie for the dinner and herded Rebecca out to the car, with Danny close behind. Just as she was closing the car door, he laid a hand on her arm. His face was quite close to hers in the dark.

"Ginny," he said.

She did not move.

"I won't bother you, I promise. I'd just like to see you now and then."

"You've already invited yourself over tomorrow morning."

"Yeah, I guess I did." Both hands were on her arms now, and he moved a little closer. "Look, you know, if you ever need anything..."

"You've said that before, Danny, and then you're gone."

"I know, I know. I'm going to stick around this time, though. I mean it."

Ginny stepped back. "Good night."

"OK." He shrugged. "I guess I can't blame you. See you in the morning."

TWO

DANNY AND JOE ARRIVED shortly after noon on Sunday, their car loaded with camera equipment and plaster for making casts. Rebecca led them down to the creek, pointing out the area where she had seen—whatever she had seen. She seemed all right today, after a good night's sleep, though she was heady with excitement over her "Bigfoot sighting" and Danny's attention.

Ginny followed them down to the creek, where Danny was flagging off a brushy area with yellow ribbon.

"Any opinions?" she asked.

Danny shook his head. "Not yet."

Rebecca hopped impatiently beside them. "What are we going to do now?"

"We're going to search the area you indicated inch by inch, just like the cops do at the scene of a crime."

Rebecca's eyes lit up. "Wow! Maybe we'll even find tracks, like in that movie."

Ginny left them a few minutes later. She crossed the small meadow that lay between the road and the creek, then paused for a moment to look at the house. She could still remember her first sight of it. They had been driving down Tenmile River Road, she and Dale, with rain streaking across the windshield. Dale had already started work at the ranger station, and she was five months pregnant. The house belonged to Holiday Acres. They had talked the Meissners into letting them move in—that was before Harriet's first husband died—then fixed it up in lieu of rent. That summer, while Dale was away on fires, Ginny had slipped Rebecca into a babypack and explored the woods. Five or six old homesteads lay along Elk Creek, the houses long gone, their foundations marked by lilac bushes and empty squares of grass outlined by daffodils. The fall that they made the down payment on the house, Ginny had dug flower bulbs up there and planted them around the porch—their porch, their house. Those had been the good times, the really good times.

Ginny got her sketch pad out and sat on the back porch, wondering about Bigfoot. They were supposed to be shy, gentle creatures, probably vegetarian, with a distinct aversion to human contact. "Smart attitude," Ginny murmured to herself as her pencil hovered over the paper. She began to draw.

Later, when the sun slipped behind the ridge and the air turned cool, she went into the house and made coffee. The others joined her in the kitchen, hot and flushed from their search. They had found a few broken twigs and some scuff marks, enough to conclude that "something big went up the creek during the past week." Nothing worth making a plaster cast of, to Rebecca's disappointment.

Ginny set a plate of cookies on the table and sat down beside her daughter. "You're really getting into this, aren't you?"

Rebecca bit into a cookie. "I'm going to ask if we can do it for our research project." A few days earlier, Galina's fourth-grade teacher had assigned her students to research teams. Rebecca's team had not yet come up with a topic.

"I'm surprised someone hasn't chosen Bigfoot already."

"Billy Geiger was talking about it, but this is different. He's never seen one."

Ginny raised an eyebrow. "No one's sure you have either."

"I'm sure." Rebecca looked up. "I'm really sure."

At last the cameras were back in the car and the men were ready to go. Ginny stepped out on the porch with Danny. The sun had already dropped behind Jackson Ridge, throwing the narrow valley into shadow. Danny laid a hand on her shoulder.

"You OK, Ginny? You look a little low."

She shrugged. "I don't know if it's good for Rebecca to get so worked up over something like this."

"Hey, she had a good time this afternoon."

"I know. I'm sorry, Danny. I know she really likes being with you. But the whole Bigfoot thing seems to appeal to, well . . ."

"Fringe elements, I believe they're called." He chuckled. "And kids. Kids are real interested in Bigfoot."

"They're real interested in dinosaurs, too, but they don't expect to catch one."

Joe came out and they were ready to go. Ginny watched them from the porch, while beside her Rebecca waved vigorously until they were out of sight.

GALINA RANGER STATION was quiet the next day, with the crew in California and another seven people gone on fire camp assignments. Early Tuesday afternoon Craig Wheeler, the head of Silviculture, stepped into Dispatch. He was in his late thirties, stocky, with thinning blond hair and a face that looked permanently sunburned. Ginny liked him. "Ranger wants to see us in his office in ten minutes."

She looked up from her desk. "Me? That's a surprise. What's up?"

"Probably some new cost-cutting scheme," Craig said. "Maybe he's going to make you the new FMO."

"Ha, ha." She waved her hand at him. "Get out of here."

"I'm going, I'm going." He stuck his head back in. "Say, you didn't ship Alvarez to California, did you?"

"No, I couldn't get hold of him. Why?"

"He didn't show up yesterday."

"He didn't call in?"

"No, and he's not here today, either."

"You know, I thought it was funny when he wasn't home on Saturday. He was so eager to go on a fire."

"You don't know what happened between him and Harriet up at Holiday Acres, do you?"

Ginny shook her head. "I just know he worked there for years. Did you talk to her before you hired him?"

"Yeah, I went up there. I never did get it clear if she fired him or he quit."

"And now you're wondering."

"Yeah. Now I'm wondering if he pulled some stunt like this."

"Could be, but I've always had the impression he was pretty responsible." What she was remembering, though, was the telephone call she had made on Saturday, the anxious woman who had answered. "You worried about him?"

"A little. Let's see if he shows up later today." Craig glanced at the clock. "Oops. We better get hopping."

They walked down the hall together. In his office, the ranger pulled up chairs for them and sat down, smiling with satisfaction. "We've got a helicopter."

"Oh?" Craig looked up. "We do?"

"All day tomorrow. Coffee Creek District had Webfoot Whirlybirds lined up to burn, but they canceled because they didn't have enough people. So now we've got a helicopter."

Ginny stared at him. Galina's ranger was known for running a cost-effective operation, and the flying torch was expensive. All summer Len had tried to talk him into using it. The district was swamped with logged units that had to be burned before they could be replanted, but the lighting crew couldn't do it all by hand. Now they finally had the helicopter, but they had the same problem as Coffee Creek.

"We don't have enough people either," she said.

The ranger smiled and handed them a crew list. Almost everyone left on the district was included. Ginny was assigned to helicopter support, something she was trained in but never got much chance to do. Craig was lined out as burn boss.

"Which unit?" Craig asked.

The ranger turned to Ginny. "What's ready to go?"

Fire Control had a half dozen units trailed, with burn plans in place. Not all of them were suitable for the flying torch, though, especially when they were short on people. "Cripple Elk," Ginny said. "We won't need so many holders."

"Cripple Elk it is." The ranger stood up. "The helicopter's due at ten A.M."

THEY BURNED on Wednesday. Late that morning Ginny watched as Ducks Wilson banked his helicopter sharply to the left, slipping drops of fire from the torch under the ship's belly. Below him the Cripple Elk unit fell away to the creek, a tinderbox of brush and slash. As Ducks pulled away from his turn, a sheet of flame whooshed up behind him. He lined the chopper up for another run.

Ginny spoke into her radio. "Good going, Ducks. One more pass through the middle, and then Wheeler says to take her out from the bottom." She and Craig Wheeler were stationed on the opposite ridge, where they had a good view of Ducks's helicopter and most of the unit.

"Ten-four. Just about ready."

"How's your fuel?"

"Still got plenty."

Ducks controlled the flow of Luma-gel from inside the ship. When the valve was open, jellied fuel dripped past an open flame, igniting before it hit the slash. Ducks loved helicopters—he was always ready to fly—and he especially loved the flying torch. Webfoot Whirlybirds did all kinds of jobs, from ferrying Christmas trees to dusting crops, but Ducks freely admitted that burning slash was the most exciting. He was lucky, he said; of all the chopper pilots he'd known in Vietnam, only two or three had flying jobs.

Lighting slash burns took skill, skill that made Ducks Galina's top choice for the job. The first couple of passes across the top established a firebreak; the next few ignited the body of the unit. That was the most dangerous part, as the heat funneled smoke and flame up into a column, creating unpredictable winds and blinding clouds of smoke. Then a final pass across the bottom, while the flames raced up the hill, sucked into the swirling column of smoke and heated air.

They were watching Ducks get ready for his next pass when Danny Meissner's car lurched to a stop behind them. Danny hopped out, followed a moment later by Joe Gilmore.

"Howdy, everyone." Danny gave Craig a mock salute, his standard greeting to anyone in Forest Service uniform.

Craig nodded, his mind on the job. "We're pretty busy right now."

"Joe wanted to stop. You can't exactly hide *that*, you know." Danny pointed at the column, rearing white against the sky, while gusts of dirty brown smoke swirled up from around its foot. The plume blotted out the sun, throwing a garish red glow over the road, the parked trucks, the darting helicopter.

Across the draw, the eerie light glinted off the hard hats of fire fighters stationed along each side of the unit, half a dozen on each line. As the heat slacked off, they would move into the burn with their hoses, wetting down the edges, putting out any spots that leapt the line.

Joe was watching with unfeigned interest. "Always did wonder what the Forest Circus needed all those people for," he said.

Ginny cocked an eyebrow at him. "I suppose you loggers would burn a unit like this with half a dozen guys."

"Shoot, two or three." Joe shifted the wad of snoose in his mouth and spit modestly off to one side.

Ginny chuckled. "What are you two doing out here, anyway?"

"We've just been out to the coast, talking to Laughing Charlie and his boys," Danny said.

"About Bigfoot."

"Of course. Old Charlie says that his grandfather's brother saw a whole family of Bigfoot somewhere on Jackson Ridge."

"That must have been a long time ago, Danny."

"Sure, but it shows that your creek was part of their original range."

Ginny kept her eyes on the helicopter. Ducks was almost finished with his pass. "Well, you better tell Rebecca. She's deep into Bigfoot research."

Ginny's radio started to chatter. She listened to Ducks for a moment, then hit the transmit switch and okayed him for the next pass.

"How is Rebecca?" Danny asked.

"On top of the world. The center of attention at school."

"I'll bet she loves it."

"Too much, but I guess it makes up for being so sick on Halloween. She wants me to ask you to dinner, by the way."

"That's not much of an invitation, but I guess I'll take what I can get."

They watched Ducks swing the helicopter into the final pass across the bottom. Luma-gel hit the slash. Nothing happened for an instant, then a fountain of flame shot into the air with a tremendous rush. Fire cracked and roared. The chopper, caught in the sudden updraft, lurched to one side. Ducks's voice exploded over the radio in a volley of swearwords as he wrenched on the stick, pulling the ship away from the fire.

Stunned, they watched the helicopter right itself and cross the draw to hover over the road a few hundred feet away.

"What the hell was that?" Ducks snapped into his mike.

Ginny lifted her radio, eyes still on the flames. "Can't tell from here."

"Took off like a goddamn funeral pyre," Ducks muttered.

Craig turned his binoculars on the area that had unexpectedly flared up. "Nothing there now. Must have been a pocket of dry stuff. Ask Ducks if he wants to finish that line."

"Whirlybird, this is Trask. Can you finish the pass?"

"I guess so," Ducks said. "Let's hope there aren't any more surprises." He swung the chopper out over the draw, hesitated for a moment, then opened the Luma-gel valve.

LATE THE NEXT DAY the first big storm of the season swept in from the Pacific, knocking down a few trees and dumping two inches of rain on the Neskanie Valley. The Cripple Elk mop-up crew, working regular days with no overtime, greeted the end of fire season with relief. The rest of Galina relaxed, too. The ranger lifted fire restrictions from the loggers and woodcutters, while the farmers started their fall plowing. In the afternoon the district got word that the crew from California would get back before ten that night.

Ginny spent the rest of the day finishing up odds and ends of work. Friday would be hectic, equipment to check in, rig vouchers to go over, time sheets to okay.

Wildfires produced a tremendous amount of paper-work, just like everything else in the government.

She was getting a file in the deserted Silviculture of-fice when Craig Wheeler's phone rang. She answered it out of habit. A man with a strong Spanish accent was on the line.

"This is Galina, *sí?* Where Nino Alvarez works? The U.S. Forest Service?"

The Cripple Elk burn had put all thoughts of Nino Alvarez right out of Ginny's head. She did not even know if Craig had tried to get hold of him. She lis-tened patiently as the man explained himself in a mix-ture of Spanish and English. He was a cousin of Alvarez's, he said. Did anyone know where Nino was?

No, she told him, no one at Galina had seen Nino all week. Nino's boss very much wanted to know where he was.

"He has not been home. And you do not know where he is?"

She assured him that she did not. At last Nino's cousin, clearly perplexed, gave up and said good-bye.

Ginny stayed in Craig's chair. Now she was wor-ried. She did not know Nino well, but because Re-becca often stayed at Holiday Acres, she knew something about him. Harriet's first husband, Wes, had hired Nino years ago, when he was just a kid who hardly spoke English. He must be, what, twenty-four or twenty-five by now, though he still looked like a boy. He was a good worker, friendly, responsible, always on time.

That was what worried her most. The Nino Alvarez she knew would either have shown up Monday morning or called. She wished Craig were there, to tell her what to do, but he was gone for a training session. The ranger wasn't in either. She picked up the phone and dialed the front desk.

"Maureen? Ginny here. What's the name of that new cop in the SO?"

There was a pause while Maureen checked. "Carver. Frank Carver. You want his number?"

Ginny took it down and hung up the phone, shaking her head. Anyone but Maureen Evans would have wondered why she wanted to call law enforcement. Maureen was just too lazy to ask. She dialed again.

"Carver here." The voice was gruff, but not unfriendly.

Ginny introduced herself and explained the situation. Carver stopped her a couple of times to ask for details, then summarized what she had told him.

"Alvarez has worked for Galina for three months. He wasn't at home on Saturday, and then didn't show up on Monday. No one's seen him all week. Why did you wait until now to get worried?"

"Well, I didn't know until Tuesday, and then we were busy burning the next day. A lot of other people are gone, too, on that California fire."

Carver grunted. "Got a home address and phone for him?"

"Just a minute." She flipped through the address file on Craig's desk and gave Carver the information.

"What's going to happen now?" she asked.

"Oh, I'll poke around a little bit, maybe come out to Galina and talk to his boss, talk to the family. I'll tell you, though, miss, I don't expect to find much. The guy's either at home or he doesn't want to be found."

"If he's not at home, will you look for him?"

"Probably not. An adult's got the right to take off if he wants to."

She hung up a moment later, less satisfied than she had hoped. Nino Alvarez might have the right to take off without telling either his boss or his family, but somehow she did not believe he would.

THREE

"LEN'S NOT a *bad* boss," Ginny said. It was Monday, the first of December, almost four weeks since the Cripple Elk burn. Ginny and Craig Wheeler were having coffee in the Silviculture office. "He's real fair on my evaluations, he gets me extra training, he even put me up for a promotion."

He had also finally learned to keep his hands to himself, she added silently. She had never imagined that Len's casual touch on her shoulder or knee had any special meaning, but she had not liked it. A few months ago she had finally asked him to stop and, to her surprise, he had.

"If he's so great," Craig asked, "why are you in here drinking coffee with me?"

"He's driving me up the wall. This morning he finally realized that I moved our files last month. So he's sitting in Dispatch, grouchy as all get out because he can't find anything."

"They're all like that in Fire Control, Ginny. They don't know what to do when they're cooped up inside."

"Make the rest of us miserable. You know what he did, first thing when he got back from California? He went right out and checked that helicopter burn. As though we didn't know what we were doing."

"Of course he wanted to check on things. He's in charge of fire, just like I'm in charge of Silviculture, and he'd been gone over a week."

"You'd think we weren't supposed to burn without him, the way he acted."

Craig shook his head. "This rain has kept us all cooped up too long. You could stand to get out into the field yourself."

Craig was right, she decided the next morning. Her boots and rain gear had spent most of the summer gathering dust in a closet. She dragged them out, gave the boots a quick coat of grease, signed up for a rig, and left the office to do a fuels survey. A day in the woods, counting sticks, would do her good.

She drove along the Neskanie highway, past the Galina mill, past Tenmile River, to the turnoff for Jackson Ridge. The truck chugged up the twisting road, through stands of timber broken by clear-cuts full of vigorous young firs. Hobson Logging had been working on the ridge for over a month now. Their watchman poked his grizzled head out of his trailer to peer at her as she drove past. A little farther along she stopped for a moment to watch the loggers, their equipment and trucks scattered like toys along the far ridge. The felled timber lay neatly crisscrossed down the slope. Above the ridgeline the yarder tower rose through the rain like a giant spike. Cables looped from it down into the unit, where loggers scrambled over the felled and bucked timber to attach the dangling chokers. Ginny watched the men scatter as a log jerked up, swinging wildly at the end of a line. Up on the ridge the yarder operator began reeling it in. He would add it to the log deck on the landing, and from there it would go to the Galina mill. The piping notes of the yarder whistle reached Ginny's ears, softened by the curtains of rain. In the distance tendrils of cloud curled among the dark, folded hills. The ranger station and Len Whittaker were over twenty miles away, and she felt just fine.

She drove on to the unit she planned to survey. Because she was out of shape from a summer at the radio, she had picked one that, on the contour map, looked reasonably flat. Not that that was saying much—they were all steep. She opened the truck door, took a deep breath, and suddenly recoiled.

Death. The damp air carried a carrion taint that made her wish she could shut her nostrils. She walked along the side of the road, taking shallow little breaths, looking. A few minutes later she found it, the body of a deer lying in the roadside ditch, belly bloated from decay. She turned away from the stench. Maybe a road kill, maybe wounded during hunting season, maybe even a natural death. Whatever it was, she did not feel like working here today.

She got back in the truck and took the map out. This finger of Jackson Ridge ended at an old fire lookout that commanded a view of the Tenmile River valley— her own house was visible from the abandoned tower, only a mile or two away as the crow flew. Over twenty to drive it, though, along roads that followed the twisting rivers and hills. She studied the map. Another unit farther along the road, part of the same sale, was also due for a fuels survey. She decided to give that one a try.

The clouds started breaking up about ten, but rain still trickled down from the canopy. Ginny struggled through the brush, her olive drab rain gear gleaming in the fitful sun. The woods were silent except for the splash and drip of falling water, the ground underfoot cushioned with moss. Rotting logs sent up wisps of steam as she clambered over them. She stopped, flagged a branch for plot center, and noted all fuels within a prescribed radius—everything from needles and twigs to snags and fallen logs. Then she beat her way through the brush for another hundred and twenty feet and did it all over again. Every now and then a cascade of drops drummed on her hard hat from a branch overhead.

She stopped for an early lunch near the bottom of the unit, not far from the creek. The firs thinned out a little here, giving way to maples and alders. A few tattered yellow leaves clung to their branches. Ginny ate her sandwich and drank cold tea, contemplating the enormous raw scar spread across the opposite hillside. It was one of that summer's burns, acres of red dirt and sodden black ashes. Charred spikes of brush stood up against the sky like skeletons. A few hemlocks and cedars remained along the creek, part of the streamside buffer left to protect the young salmon. Beneath them the tangled brush gave way to spots of bare ground covered with a litter of needles and cones.

A good place to look for mushrooms. Dale had loved the big yellow chanterelles that Galina was famous for—he liked to cook them with chicken in a special sauce. Suddenly the great, empty feeling swept over her again, unpredictable as always. Dale walking ahead of her through the woods with Rebecca, still a baby, asleep in the backpack, her face nestled against the back of his neck. Dale at the kitchen sink, washing dishes. Dale kissing her good-bye that last morning, saying he might be late.

She held herself still, willing the images to stop. She did not need to remember it all again, the phone call, the hospital, the doctor gently leading her from Dale's room. She kept her eyes focused, instead, on a patch of brush across the creek. She was not really looking at the gnarled, moss-draped vine maple, not really seeing it, but the effort kept the other visions at bay. Slowly the emptiness passed and she found herself staring at something bright among the fallen leaves, something red.

There shouldn't be anything red. Ginny stretched up on her toes and peered into the shadows, then sat back down.

A heavy sick feeling settled in her stomach. Of course, she couldn't really tell, not from this far away. Maybe it wasn't a red cap. Anyway, lots of people wore red caps.

She didn't want to look. Maybe she could just call Len on the truck radio—sure, get him all the way out here to look at an old hat some hunter had lost. No, this was something she was going to have to do herself.

She got up and pushed through the tangled salmonberry to the creek, waded across, and climbed up the other side. The cap was lying a few yards from the bank. She got close enough to see the words written across the front. Holiday Acres. Everyone who worked there wore one. She forced herself to examine the area. Scraps of cloth lay scattered over the ground, their red plaid almost lost in the mud. Extending from one of the scraps was a hand. Two of the fingers were missing.

She lurched back to the creek and knelt there until her stomach stopped heaving. She filled her hard hat with water, splashed some on her face, rinsed her mouth out, then rummaged through her pockets for a roll of flagging. Without a backward glance she tore a piece off, tied it to one of the cedars, crossed the creek, and took off up the hill, leaving a trail of yellow ribbon.

FORTY MILES AWAY, at the Neskanie Supervisor's Office in Longmont, Frank Carver was just settling down at his desk after lunch. He eyed the disorderly stack of papers piled in his in-basket. Most of them had to do with the marijuana-eradication campaign that had ended in November. The Forest Service, the county sheriff's office, and the state police had joined forces to find and destroy pot plantations. After ten years in vice and narcotics in Seattle, Frank had found it a change to be in on this end of things.

His lunch sat heavily in his stomach. If he ate salads and started working out at the gym, he might lose the rubber tire developing around his middle. Not that he was in bad shape, not for a man just past fifty. He just didn't like salad. He turned his contemplation to the wet cars in the parking lot outside. What he really wanted to do was go fishing. The rains had brought the Neskanie up high enough for the first big run of salmon to make it past the tidewater mark, and the river was thick with drift boats. A day like today would be perfect. He closed his eyes and thought about the boat one of the SO engineers had for sale. She was a beauty, freshly caulked and painted, and the price included a trailer. He could name her the Minnie, after his former wife. She had always hated that nickname and insisted on Minerva. Even in bed.

He opened his eyes and stared glumly at the papers. Finally he stuck his hand in the pile, pulled a sheet out from the middle, and got to work.

He was still at it when the telephone rang and Len Whittaker's voice came on. Frank had met Len briefly, just long enough to sense that the Galina FMO had to work at being friendly. Today his voice was quick and a little high, the words tumbling out.

"A body in the woods. She didn't get too close, and she didn't want to say much on the radio, but she's sure."

Frank fumbled with a pencil, broke the tip, and reached for a pen. "Is she still out there?"

"...waiting for us. She flagged her way out."

Frank finally got the pen to work, cursing his sudden clumsiness. "Has anyone called the sheriff's office?"

"Not yet. The ranger told me to report to you right away."

"OK," Frank said, getting control of himself. "I'll be in Galina in forty minutes. I'll need someone to show me where she is. The most important thing is that nobody goes near the body. Got that?"

"Ten-four."

Frank hung up. He hoped to God it wasn't a girl. Five years ago, he had been the first to get to Sheila's body, after the phone call. He had not been quick enough, though, to keep Paul—his partner, Sheila's father—from seeing. The look on his face. Frank never wanted to see that look again, on anyone.

They had been close, very close, to destroying a major Seattle drug gang. Then Sheila had been murdered, and her body left as a warning, in a public park. It had taken a year to bring the two killers to trial, their lawyers delaying at every step, but finally they were there, in court, at the defendants' table. Paul had been taken off the case long before, but no one could keep him out of the courtroom. He was there every day.

Then one morning, he walked up the aisle, past the spectators and reporters, pulled a gun out of his pocket, and calmly shot both men.

They were dead now, and Paul was in a psychiatric ward, though Frank privately considered him no crazier than anyone else. He sat at his desk for a moment, going over a mental checklist of what he would need. Most of it was already in his rig. Collecting evidence was pretty much the same, whether the evidence was for timber theft or homicide. Then he pulled himself up short. He had no reason to think this was a homicide.

He notified the county sheriff, who promised to send an ambulance and then go out there himself. On his way out he stopped by Larry Hunsaker's office. The forest supervisor wasn't in. Frank wrote a note, folded the paper in half, and gave it to the secretary. Her eyebrows were already going up as he went out the door. The whole office would know within twenty minutes.

He made it to Galina in half an hour, taking the narrow, twisting Mouse Mountain road faster than he ever had before. Len Whittaker was waiting in the parking lot. He piled his boots and rain gear into Frank's rig, and they pulled back out onto the highway.

The FMO sounded a little calmer than he had on the telephone. "Sheriff Holt called to say the ambulance will take awhile. He and his deputy are on their way."

Frank nodded and adjusted the volume on his police scanner. The county dispatcher was giving directions to an auto accident, and on the CB a couple of truckers made plans to stop for coffee. There was a Forest Service radio too, and a mobile phone. Getting behind the wheel made Frank feel like he was in a science-fiction movie.

"Anyone call the medical examiner?" Frank asked.

"I don't know. Why?"

"Someone's got to declare the corpse dead. Who's the ME around here, anyway?"

"Someone from the hospital, I guess."

Len sank into silence after that, except to give directions. Frank left him alone. The county sheriff would have put the standard routine into motion. Frank stretched his fingers out and wrapped them back around the steering wheel. The river running alongside looked mighty good—high and fast, but not too muddy. He glanced enviously at a couple of fishermen, their boat rocking gently near the bank.

They took the road up Jackson Ridge, following it along the top of the Elk Creek drainage. The watchman for Hobson Logging popped his head out of the trailer as they went by, eyes avid with curiosity. Len gave him a friendly wave.

Sheriff Holt, a heavyset man with thin, gray hair, was waiting for them. He leaned against the side of his patrol car, staring gloomily at the trees. He waited until they had parked, then walked over.

"Deputy Wilcox is already down there with your gal. Doc Jarvis is on his way."

Frank got out. "Any idea when he'll get here?"

"It'll be awhile." The sheriff thumbed his radio. "Wilcox? We're heading down. Anything you need?"

"No, sir." The deputy's voice sounded thin and reedy. "Mrs. Trask is pretty cold, though."

"I've got a blanket." Frank opened the back of the rig and got his pack out. Inside was the kit he had carried through most of his career, a black leather case holding an assortment of bottles and bags, tweezers, calipers, magnifying glasses, dusting powder and brushes. Tucked away in a pocket, next to his camera, was a small bottle of whiskey. He added a blanket to the pack, shrugged it up onto his shoulders, locked the doors, and followed Len Whittaker and the sheriff over the side of the road.

The brush was dense, resistant, reaching out to snag and trip them. Frank lowered his head and bulldozed through, shaking loose enough water to drench his neck and shoulders. He stopped to unwrap a blackberry vine from his foot while Len scanned the mass of green for the next yellow ribbon.

Sheriff Holt joined them, breathing hard. He shouted down the hill, got an answering call from Wilcox, and they set off again, Len leading the way around the worst of the brush. Frank stumbled after him, catching his feet every other step and marveling at the FMO's surefootedness.

Ginny sat huddled on a fallen log, listening to them push their way downhill. Jimmy Wilcox had loaned her his jacket, but even with that wrapped around her shoulders and her raingear on top she was shivering. It was past two o'clock, almost three hours since she had found the body. She had scrambled out of the unit, radioed in to Len, then waited in the truck until Wilcox showed up. Surely they would let her go home now. She wanted coffee, a hot bath, and then sleep in her own bed, with Rebecca in the next room.

Len was the first across the creek. She looked up hopefully as he came toward her and laid a hand on her shoulder.

"You OK, Ginny? I called Susie and sent her over to your place."

She nodded. She was usually home by three forty-five, when the school bus dropped Rebecca off, and she was grateful that someone would be there to meet her daughter. "Can I go now?"

But Len was already starting up the hill to join the sheriff and Frank Carver. Ginny pulled the jacket tighter and got up. Their voices, hushed but warm, alive, drew her closer. Anything was better than sitting in the cold, imagining horrors worse than what was really there.

"Looks like the varmints got at him pretty good," Sheriff Holt said. "Coyotes, most likely."

Frank surveyed the few square yards of hillside littered with human remains. It wasn't like last time—last time he had recognized the victim, and had guessed at the pain and grief they were in for. He had no such feeling about these anonymous scraps of flesh and bone.

He unslung his pack and opened it. The blanket lay on top. He turned and identified Ginny Trask, remembering her voice on the phone a month earlier, when she had reported Nino Alvarez missing. She was hanging back a little, clutching herself to keep warm. "Sheriff," he asked quietly, "could you get started here? I'd like to talk to the young lady."

Frank took Ginny's arm and walked her down the hill to a fallen log where they could sit looking across the creek while Holt and his deputy worked. He introduced himself, gently removed her rain jacket, and tucked the blanket around her shoulders. She looked like a kid, skinny, her dark hair in an unruly mop, her face stripped raw by rain and shock. He handed her the flask of whiskey.

She choked a mouthful down. "I've talked to you before."

"About a month ago. I remember. More whiskey?"

She shook her head.

"OK, now. Tell me what happened."

She did a good job, keeping her story brief and to the point. She faltered only when she got to the cap. He helped her there, asking why that was important.

"Because then I knew who it was."

"And who do you think it is?"

"Nino Alvarez. The one I called you about. He always wore a Holiday Acres cap." Her shoulders started shaking again, and she closed her eyes for a moment.

He waited. Had she and Alvarez been close? He didn't think so—he would have picked up some hint of it while investigating the man's disappearance. Most likely she was upset by finding the body.

Ginny wiped her eyes with a crumpled bandanna. "I just keep remembering the last time I saw Nino, in the Galina store. He was buying a book, a little kid's book."

"A book," Frank repeated.

"*The Velveteen Rabbit*. We've got it at home." She looked up. Her gray eyes were clear, and she seemed composed again. "Now I wonder why he wanted a little kid's book."

"Maybe for his daughter."

"His daughter? I didn't know he had a daughter."

"He has a wife and two girls."

Sheriff Holt had been busy on the radio while they talked. Now he and Deputy Wilcox came down to join them. "Len Whittaker thinks it's Alvarez."

Frank nodded. "So does Mrs. Trask."

"Not much for us to do here, then," the sheriff said. "Federal employee on federal land would be your jurisdiction."

Frank nodded again, guessing from the sheriff's reluctance what would come next.

"We can stay till Doc Jarvis comes."

"I'm going to need some help searching the area."

Sheriff Holt shrugged. "Maybe the ambulance crew can help out."

GINNY TRAILED after them as they moved back up the hill. Nino had children. Had anyone at the station known that? She didn't think so. No one at Holiday Acres had ever mentioned it either, and he had worked there for years. The woman who had answered the phone that afternoon, her voice so worried—that must have been his wife. Ginny swallowed.

"So this is where Alvarez ended up," Len said. He and Ginny watched as Sheriff Holt held a ruler beside a scrap of cloth. Frank snapped his camera, and they moved to another spot a few feet away. "I wonder what he was doing down here."

"Growing pot, most likely." The sheriff knelt down with a grunt, then glanced at Ginny. "Say now, how would you like to hold this ruler? Just put it where Carver says, and don't step on anything important."

Ginny took over while the sheriff got to his feet. They were almost done when the ambulance crew came crashing through the brush, followed by Doc Jarvis. The medical examiner, a thin, grouchy man in his sixties, was clearly not happy about being out in the woods.

"So this is it?" Jarvis glanced around. "You don't need me to tell you he's dead. Maybe I'll know more after the lab work."

Frank took a couple more pictures and got the ambulance crew started. Sheriff Holt and his deputy left with Doc Jarvis. Frank looked at his watch. It was after three, and the daylight was already starting to fade. He turned to Len and Ginny.

"I could use some help searching the area."

"I'll stay," Len said promptly. "Ginny can take her rig in now, and I'll ride back with you."

"Mrs. Trask?"

Ginny looked up. Staying would make her late, but Rebecca would be OK with Susie there. She appreciated the way Frank Carver let Len know that the choice was hers. Perhaps that was what made up her mind. She nodded slowly. "I'd like to stay."

They moved out from the flagged area in a spiral pattern, examining the ground. Of course, Frank thought, they weren't trained detectives, but they did know the forest floor. Anything that didn't belong would stick right out. Two hours of search turned up three more bones, a few more scraps of cloth, and a grisly skull. Frank found it. Ginny and Len both came running at his call. Ginny took one look and turned away, sick to her stomach. She was glad that Len was helping, so she wouldn't have to see it again.

Frank seemed pleased. "Should get a positive ID off this," he told them.

Dusk came early in the deep little canyon, a drizzle set in, and by five o'clock they were ready to go home.

Ginny was making a final sweep near the edge of the burned unit when she found the shoe, a canvas sneaker discolored by the weather but otherwise almost new. She called the others over. Frank took a couple of pictures, then gently dislodged the shoe from its resting place, revealing a piece of black plastic. He took a picture of that, too. As he worked the plastic loose from the mud, a jumble of twigs and needles fell to the ground. Len brushed them away while Frank slipped the shoe into an evidence bag.

They got up and stood for a moment, looking at the dismal landscape. The drizzle was picking up, turning into rain; already the tops of the trees had vanished into the dusk. Frank tucked everything into his pack and shrugged it up on his shoulders.

"Let's get out of here," he said. "We're done."

FOUR

AT 10:00 A.M. the next morning Frank Carver waited in the forest supervisor's office, turning a Styrofoam coffee cup between his hands. Every now and then he glanced dolefully at the report on Hunsaker's desk. He had been rehearsing what he planned to say since writing it four hours ago, but he still did not feel ready. What he felt was exhausted, and jittery from too much caffeine.

Last night he had driven the thirty miles to Harmony, the little Willamette Valley town where the Alvarez family lived. He had been there almost a month earlier, when Nino was first reported missing. The two Alvarez brothers, stocky, dark men in their early thirties, had greeted him with even more suspicion than they had shown on his first visit. Felicia Alvarez, Nino's wife, had stared at him as he broke the news, then turned and rushed out of the room. Frank did not think she knew much English, but she had obviously understood.

On his way back to Longmont, he had stopped in Salem to check with the state police about Alvarez's car. There was still no response to the tracer he had put on it as part of the earlier investigation. He had spent the small hours of the morning writing his report, then caught a couple hours of sleep before this meeting with Hunsaker and Sheriff Holt.

The forest supervisor was making conversation while they waited for the sheriff. Larry Hunsaker was in his late fifties, a trim, athletic man with a deeply seamed face, brown hair touched with gray around the edges, and a talent for internal politics. His eyes followed Frank's gaze to the report.

"I don't mind telling you, Frank, I had my doubts when we created the law enforcement position. What do we need a cop for? I asked myself. Right now, though, I'm damned glad you're on board."

Frank nodded. Of course Hunsaker felt that way. Better a man who had been on the team for even a few months than some specially assigned honcho out of the regional office in Portland or, worse yet, Washington, DC.

There was a tap on the door, and Hunsaker's secretary looked in. "Sheriff Holt is here. He went down to Fire Control for a cup of coffee."

"Have him come right in when he gets back. Anything else?"

"Two calls from Wilson at the *Herald-Tribune*."

Hunsaker groaned. "Why are these reporters so damned efficient? What does he want?"

"He wants to know what's going on out in Galina. So do the rest of us."

Hunsaker glanced at Frank. "We're not quite sure yet."

''Here's the sheriff.'' Her face disappeared from the doorway, and Holt came in. He nodded to Hunsaker, then to Frank, and sat down. He looked as though he had not had much sleep either.

Hunsaker cleared his throat. ''Finding the body on federal land was bad enough, but this...'' He tapped Frank's report. ''I don't suppose there's any other possibility?''

Frank shook his head. ''Not that I can see.''

Hunsaker glanced at the sheriff.

''I'd never claim Doc Jarvis is perfect,'' Sheriff Holt said, ''but he does a good, thorough autopsy. If he says the cause of death was probably a blow to the skull, I believe it.''

''Murdered.'' Hunsaker took a minute to give the back of his neck a thorough rub. ''This man, Nino Alvarez—we don't know for sure it's him?''

''Not yet,'' Frank said. ''We're having the dental records checked.''

''It's him,'' said the sheriff, shifting in his chair.

''Let's assume it is, then,'' Hunsaker continued. ''He was a Forest Service employee. Had he been with us long?''

''About four months,'' Frank said.

''Did he die on Forest Service land?''

''If you mean out there where we found him, probably not. The body appears to have been wrapped in black plastic and dumped.''

The sheriff nodded. ''Little bits of plastic all over.''

''So he could have been killed anywhere?''

"In theory," Frank replied. "But he was last seen in Galina."

"At the ranger station," the sheriff added. He had also read Frank's report. "Federal property. The kid was staying up at the station."

Frank grunted. Sheriff Holt didn't want the case either, and he didn't blame him. He ran over his prepared lines again: A case like this requires the resources of a fully equipped law enforcement agency. This isn't forest arson or contract fraud. Of course, I'll be glad to cooperate with Sheriff Holt . . .

"I talked to the DA this morning," the sheriff was saying. "We both tend to the idea that with Alvarez being a federal employee, and found on federal land, this is your case. Of course, I'll do everything I can to cooperate with Agent Carver . . ."

Frank listened with growing dismay. "A case like this," he began, but Sheriff Holt was not to be interrupted.

"We don't have much in the way of a crime lab. Generally we send everything up to the state lab in Salem. There shouldn't be any problem with Carver doing the same. And he can borrow Deputy Wilcox now and then. I can't spare him more than a few hours a week—there's just three of us for the whole county. So you see, we'd all consider it a favor if you'd take the thing off our hands."

"Homicide isn't part of a special agent's duties," Frank said, making a last try.

"But you're not just any special agent," the sheriff pointed out. "Not with ten years on the Seattle narcotics squad. I'd guess you've personally investigated more homicides than this county has seen in the last hundred years."

Hunsaker turned to Frank, clearly surprised at his reluctance. "What do you say, Frank?"

"If you assign me to the case, I'll do my best."

Hunsaker nodded. "All right, Sheriff, I'll give the DA a call."

Sheriff Holt heaved himself to his feet. "That's a load off my mind. We've got three drunks in the jail, and just before I left Wilcox went out on a burglary call. I need a homicide like I need a hole in the head."

After the sheriff had gone, Hunsaker considered his new law enforcement officer. "What's the problem, Frank? I'd think you'd be pawing the ground to get started."

Frank looked up. "No problem." He had promised himself, when he left Seattle, that he would keep away from death and violence. He had pictured himself investigating misuse of government property. And now this.

"The way I read the regulations, Frank, you're in charge of any major crime involving a Forest Service employee."

"With a little help from Deputy Wilcox."

"As little as possible, from the sound of it. You *are* going to need a hand, though, and Holt isn't the only one with a personnel shortage." Hunsaker tipped his

chair back. "Whittaker? He's had some arson training, but I don't think so. He didn't much favor creating your job. Ha, I've got it. Ginny Trask."

Frank looked up. "The gal who found the body?"

"She's available, she knows the area, and she's been
through level-two law enforcement training."

"I haven't asked for an assistant."

Hunsaker let his chair down with a little thump.
"Well, you're getting one."

GINNY WALKED INTO Len Whittaker's office just as he
was hanging up the phone. She laid a handful of
budget forms on his desk. "Looks like the ranger
okayed that new tanker."

Len was looking at her oddly, as though she were not
quite there. She waved a hand in front of his face.
"Hello, hello?"

He gave a little jerk. "That was the SO. You've been
detailed to law enforcement."

"What?" She sat down.

"You're supposed to help Frank Carver in his investigation. He's on his way out." Len glanced at his
watch. "Should be here in half an hour."

"Can they do that? Detail me without even asking?"

"According to regulations. If they want you, you
go."

"We've got a million things to do, Len."

"We'll get by. Maureen can pick up the slack."

Maureen Evans, the receptionist, was the dispatch backup. Ginny did not think much of her abilities, but she could tell Len had already made up his mind. She sat for a moment, getting used to the idea.

"Did they say what I'll be doing?"

Len shook his head. "They said Carver's going to need a desk with locking drawers and a telephone."

In the end, Ginny gave up her own desk. It was in the cubbyhole of an office behind Dispatch, and two of the drawers had a key. She moved her papers out, tracked down a spare phone, and was plugging it in when Frank Carver arrived.

He set his briefcase on the desk and glanced around. There was just room for himself, Ginny, and one more person in the office. Big enough. He gave Ginny a critical look. He saw now that he had been wrong in thinking she was just a kid—she must be close to thirty, thin, but with nice round hips that had been hidden yesterday by her rain gear. Her hair was combed, her clothes were clean, and now that she had some color in her face she looked a lot better.

"The office door locks, too," Ginny said, "and I can probably get a clock."

"What about a typewriter?"

"There's one in Dispatch. We can move it in, if you want."

"Not right now. You do type?"

She nodded, dismayed. Was he always this grouchy?

Frank sat down at the desk and motioned her to take a seat. "We'll have lots of typing. Hunsaker says you've been through level two?"

"Last year."

"Did they cover investigative techniques?"

"Not really. It was mostly patrolling and ticket writing."

Frank leaned back in his chair. Before leaving the SO he had checked Ginny's personnel file, looking for some sort of experience he could use. He had trained quite a few cops over the years, but all of them had at least been through college. Ginny Trask had dropped out after two years as an art major. It did not look promising.

"Did they talk about observation?"

Ginny shook her head.

"Observation is a cop's best tool. When you were searching yesterday, you used your powers of observation. You're familiar with the woods. When something was out of place, like that tennis shoe, you spotted it." He paused and lifted an eyebrow. "You want to say something?"

"A shoe would be hard to miss."

"Granted." He met her eyes, but failed to find any sarcasm. "The point is that I need your ability to observe. We're going to be talking to a lot of people, people you know and I don't. I'm going to want your opinions on them, and on what they say. Got it?"

"Ten-four."

"OK. The first thing I'd like your opinion on is the food at the Galina café."

His mouth stayed deadpan, but his eyes were smiling. Ginny relaxed just a little. "They make good hamburgers."

"Are they open all night?"

"Nothing in Galina is open all night." She frowned as the full import of his question sank in. "Are we going to be working all night?"

"We're here for the duration."

But what about my kid? she silently demanded. She bit her lip. This wasn't the first time she had bumped into the unwritten rule that the job came first, the family second.

"I'll have to get a baby-sitter."

Frank did not seem to hear her. He opened the desk drawer and pulled out a notepad. "I'd like you to make a few phone calls. We'll need to check with the lab in Salem, find out how to get stuff up there. I've got some questions for Sheriff Holt, too..."

An hour later Ginny was still on the telephone. An afternoon lull had settled over the station, broken by the rustle of papers from Frank's desk and the routine murmur of radio traffic. Outside the rain drizzled down from the low gray clouds. Water dripped from the eaves as the phone rang on and on in her ear. She had called the Salem lab twice, tried three different baby-sitters, left a message for Sheriff Holt, and arranged for Rebecca to spend the afternoon with a friend who rode on the same school bus; now she was trying to reach her sister-in-law on the coast.

She hung up and tried Alice's work number. This time she got through. "Sea Haven Gifts and Curios," said Alice in the cloying voice required by her employer.

Ginny explained her predicament.

"I thought you usually got Susie Meissner."

"We do, but this could go on for days. I need someone to stay at the house. I know it's a big favor, Alice, but I'm desperate."

"Hey, no problem. It's dead out here, now that winter's started, and Bud took off for Alaska last week. I'll be glad to do it."

Bud Trask, Alice's husband, spent part of the year off the Alaska Coast on a commercial fishing boat. Ginny sighed with relief.

"Just one thing," Alice said. "I get to take Rebecca shopping at the Longmont Mall."

"Done." Alice loved to shop. As they were arranging details, Ginny heard the scrape of Frank's chair from the office. When she hung up and turned around, he was standing in the doorway, a sheaf of papers clutched in one hand.

"What is this?" he demanded. "That's at least the third personal call you've made."

"I said I had to get a baby-sitter."

"It takes you all afternoon?"

Suddenly her temper flared. "Look, I stayed out till after dark last night, helping you. I get here this morning and all of a sudden I'm working for you. No warning, no chance to make arrangements, no one even asking if I *want* to work for you.''

Frank raised his hands. ''Hey, sorry, sorry.''

''Then I find out I might be here all night. Who cares if I've got a family?'' She glared at him. ''If you don't like it, get someone else.''

''Whoa, now. No need to fly off the handle.''

Her shoulders started to shake, and for a moment she was afraid she would burst into tears in front of him. ''You aren't exactly sweetness and light, yourself.''

''No,'' Frank said, watching her. ''No, I'm afraid I'm not.''

LATER THAT AFTERNOON Frank interviewed Craig Wheeler in the little office. He had talked to Craig, who had been Alvarez's supervisor, during the initial investigation. Craig had been the last to see Alvarez the night he disappeared.

''Just the same stuff I told you before.'' Craig shifted uncomfortably in his chair and appealed to Ginny. ''I wonder now if I should have done something.''

Ginny kept her eyes on her notebook. Was she supposed to take that down? Frank had told her not to try getting everything verbatim. Concentrate on what the witness says, he told her. They could fill in the questions later, when they typed the notes up.

''What could you have done?'' Frank asked.

"Maybe I should have reported him missing that Monday, when he didn't show up for work. Hell, I don't know. Maybe I *should* have had a beer with him."

Frank raised an eyebrow. "What's this?"

"Nino asked if I wanted to stop at the tavern. It was that Friday, after work. I was on my way up to the parking lot, and he was packing his car."

"When I talked with you last month, you didn't mention beer."

Craig shrugged. "I never stop at the tavern."

"But Alvarez might have?"

"I guess."

"OK. You said he was packing his car. What was he packing it with?"

"The usual stuff he took home on weekends. A suitcase and a bag of laundry. He had the trunk open."

Frank glanced at his notes from the previous interview, when all he had been investigating was a missing employee. "That was a 1975 orange Datsun 510?"

Craig nodded. "Real beat-up."

"And you assumed he was going home. Home being Harmony."

"That's what he did every weekend."

"He'd worked for you about three months, hadn't he?"

Craig nodded. "He came on August first."

Frank checked his notes again. "He'd worked for Mrs. Whittaker at Holiday Acres before that. Why did he leave?"

Craig shrugged. "I don't know exactly. He and Harriet had a run-in over something. When he applied for the job here I went and talked to her. She wanted me to hire him."

Ginny's pencil flashed across the page and came to a stop. "One more thing," Frank said. "Did Alvarez have any enemies?"

Craig looked startled.

"Anyone who really disliked him. Dislike's not a reason to kill someone, of course, but there's usually something behind it." Craig was listening, all right. Frank pushed on. "The reason might help us get a handle on why someone did kill him."

"I don't know." Craig shook his head. "I guess anyone could have people who don't like him."

Frank waited, but that, apparently, was all he was going to get. "All right, Mr. Wheeler, thanks for going over this again. Let me know if you remember anything else."

"Sure." Craig stood up. "I still feel like I should have done something."

AT FIVE O'CLOCK the parking lot at the Galina tavern was already filled with cars and pickups gleaming softly in the rain. Frank opened the door, letting out a gust of overheated air and country music. He and Ginny paused to let their eyes adjust to the dim light. Five or six loggers, their work clothes grimy with mud, sat at the bar along one side of the narrow room. A line of booths, most of them full, ran down the other side. At the far end an overhead lamp cast a smoky haze on a couple of pool tables.

Rosie Loomis, the owner's daughter, stood behind the bar. "Hey, Ginny. Beer?"

"Not today, Rosie, thanks. This is Frank Carver, from the SO. He's trying to find out what happened to Nino Alvarez."

The two nearest loggers looked up but didn't say anything. Frank headed for a spot farther down the bar. Rosie paused to draw another beer for a customer, then joined them.

"Did Alvarez come in much?" Frank asked.

"Every couple of weeks, maybe. He wasn't a regular."

"Was he here on Friday night, October thirty-first?"

"Hell, I don't know." Rosie gave him a quizzical look. "That was over a month ago."

"Halloween night."

She thought for a moment. "I was working that night. We had a lot of people in. We give a free beer to anyone in costume on Halloween."

"Alvarez might have come pretty early," Frank said.

Rosie hesitated, thinking. "Yeah, he was here. About five. We had some Forest Service regulars, and he stopped to talk to them. I remember thinking he was working there now."

"Who were they?"

"Let's see, the usual bunch." Rosie mentioned a few names, and Ginny took them down. Three guys who carpooled in from Longmont, and a couple of locals.

"He sat near the end of the bar," Rosie said. "He had three beers."

"You've got a good memory. Was that a lot?"

"For him it was. The other times he just had one and then left."

"So he was here awhile."

"Maybe an hour."

Frank nodded and slowly looked around. He came back to Rosie. "Did he talk to anyone else?"

"Yes," Rosie said, as though she had been waiting for the question. "Maureen Evans was at the table with the Forest Service guys. She went over to Nino and talked to him for a minute. I thought at first she was trying to pick him up. But I guess not, because she went back and sat down again."

"Did they leave at the same time?"

Rosie shook her head. "I didn't notice. We get pretty busy about five thirty, especially on a Friday."

THEY LEFT the tavern and drove back to the ranger station. Frank glanced at Ginny, who was staring out the window at the rain and the fading light. Any other trainee would have been full of talk, examining what they had just learned, guessing at the next step. Not this one, though. Since the scene over the baby-sitter a couple of hours ago she had hardly said a word. He kept feeling he ought to apologize, but he was not sure how to begin.

Ginny helped him gas the truck. She had surprised herself, flaring up at him like that. In the five years she had worked for Len Whittaker she had never done such a thing, though Len had occasionally given her far more provocation. She was even more surprised to find that she actually liked Frank Carver. He was a little brusque, perhaps, but he treated her like a real person, not just another fixture behind the radio. She would have liked to ask if he had learned anything at the tavern, what they might do next, but she was afraid to open her mouth.

"Will Maureen Evans still be in?" Frank asked.

"She got off at five. We passed her on the highway." Ginny had guessed that he would want to talk to Maureen next. She smiled, pleased that she had guessed right.

They went into the office. Frank took his coat off, sat down at the desk, and began to shuffle papers. Ginny checked the clock. Five thirty. She was hungry. What would Frank want to do next? She glanced over at him, but he seemed absorbed in his papers.

She coughed, pointedly.

Frank looked up. "What are you doing here? It's almost dinnertime."

"Look, I'm sorry I yelled at you this afternoon."

"It's OK." He paused. "Well, aren't you going home?"

"Are we done for the day?"

"As done as we're going to get. What's your usual time in the morning?"

"Seven."

"OK. See you at seven."

FIVE

GINNY TOOK THE LAST turn on Tenmile Road and gave
a little start. There were lights in the windows. Of
course—Alice was there. She pulled the car into its accustomed spot near the back porch. They would have
heard the car, would be expecting her to walk through
the door in just a minute. She swallowed, hard. Suddenly it was all too much, and one of the tears she had
been holding back through the drive home dribbled
down her cheek.

It should be Dale coming home to those lighted
windows, and she should be inside, cooking dinner,
waiting for his step. It should be Dale ready to com-
plain about his boss and then, once the pressure was
off, laughing at his own complaints. Dale, Dale, Dale.
Five years. "God help me," she murmured.

Light spilled out onto the porch. The screen door
slammed, then Rebecca was opening the car door,
peering inside.

"Mom! Mom! Aunt Alice is here! And we're going
to the mall!"

Ginny got her gear out, surreptitiously wiping her
eyes on her sleeve, and followed Rebecca inside. The
kitchen was a blur of light, warmth, and steamy windows. Then Alice was taking her things, settling her on

the old sofa beside the stove, getting her a cup of coffee.

"You've really been through the wringer, haven't you?" Alice sat down beside her. "Rebecca told me how you found that poor man's body."

Ginny gave a wan smile. "I'm afraid I've been feeling a little sorry for myself."

"Well, of course you have." Alice could be tremendously comforting at times like this. "Out in the wet and cold all day, and then, after a shock like that, they don't even give you time off."

"Are you really going to find out who killed him?" Rebecca asked.

"Now, that's enough, Rebecca," said Alice. "You've had too much excitement already."

"I suppose the news is all over town," Ginny said.

Alice nodded. "I stopped at the Mercantile for a few groceries, and everyone was full of it."

"At school, too," Rebecca added. "It's been great. First I see a Bigfoot and then my own mother finds a murdered body!"

"Weren't you setting the table, Rebecca?"

"But Aunt Alice..."

"You'd better do what your aunt says," said Ginny. "And yes, I've been assigned to help the new law enforcement agent." She sank back into the couch and sat there, sipping coffee, while Alice and Rebecca put dinner on the table. It wasn't like having Dale there, but, then again, it wasn't so bad, letting someone take care of you. The warmth from the stove made her drowsy, so that she was almost asleep when Alice called her to eat.

Later that night, after Rebecca had gone to bed, Ginny helped Alice with the dishes. "So what's this Frank Carver like?" Alice asked, slipping a plate into the rinse water.

"Older—he must be fifty. He wears a real hat, like a detective in an old movie. Hardly anyone wears hats, do they?"

"Not around here. But what's he like, Ginny? You know what I mean."

"He's grouchy, I can tell you that. He yelled at me for talking to you on the phone."

"He what? That took a lot of nerve. I hope you yelled right back."

Ginny smiled. "As a matter of fact, I did."

They stacked the clean plates in the cupboard. "Danny Meissner called."

"What did he want?"

"To talk to you. I told him you were late getting home, and you'd be too tired to talk to anyone tonight."

Of course, sometimes Alice could take care of her *too* well. "You don't need to do that. Danny and Nino Alvarez were friends. He's probably just concerned about me."

"Danny Meissner has no business being concerned about you." Alice turned to look at her sister-in-law. "Does he?"

Ginny shrugged uncomfortably. "We've known the Meissners for years. They knew Dale, too."

"I don't know what you see in him. *Especially* after being married to Dale."

Ginny winced. "I haven't gone out with Danny for more than a year."

"That man is a waste of time. I can't even tell what he lives on. Harriet can't be supporting him anymore, but he came back from California with a brand-new car, *after* getting fired..."

"Oh. I didn't know he'd been fired." Alice had apparently hooked right into the local gossip. "Danny's not really so bad. He's been a good friend to me, especially after Dale died."

"Oh, sure, he came over and mowed the lawn once or twice."

"And Rebecca has always liked him."

"That whole crew out there at Holiday Acres..."

"I know, Alice. I know," Ginny said wearily. She opened the refrigerator and took out things to make a sandwich for her lunch.

"You sit down. I'll do that." Alice pushed her gently toward the table. "I don't mean to run down a friend of yours. Danny's got some good points, and I know he's always been great with Rebecca."

Ginny sat at the kitchen table. Like everyone else in Galina, when she thought of Holiday Acres she thought of Harriet—strong, domineering, the most independent woman in the valley. She had pretty much run her first husband's life. A lot of people had been surprised when she had married Len Whittaker last year, Len who always made jokes about women's lib. Then there was Susie, shy and awkward, hiding from life in romance novels and her mother's kitchen. Danny seemed different, until you got to know him. Then you saw the similarities, the self-doubts and immaturity. Two grown-up children who had never really left home.

"Will you want a thermos of coffee in the morning?" Alice asked. "Bud always takes one out on the boat."

"They have coffee at the station," Ginny said absently. "Not that it's any good." Suddenly she thought of Frank Carver. Had anyone fixed supper for him tonight? Was anyone fussing around, giving him orders and making him feel like part of the family? She didn't think so.

"Maybe I could take that extra coffeepot we got last Christmas," she said. "And some real coffee."

Alice nodded approvingly. "I'll get them out."

"Another cup, too. And a box of sugar cubes."

GINNY WAS BUSY at her typewriter the next morning when Len Whittaker called to say he would be late. "Harriet's taking Susie into town for some doctor's appointment, so I figured I'd better stay here to look after things." He had been spending a lot of time at Holiday Acres since the Christmas tree harvest had started.

"Ten-four," Ginny said. "I'll let Maureen know, too."

"How'd it go yesterday with Carver?"

"OK, I guess."

"Any leads on Alvarez?"

"He stopped at the tavern Halloween night. That's about all."

They hung up and Ginny went back to her typing. Frank had planned to stop at the SO that morning. He finally trudged in a little before eight-thirty. "Fog's so thick out there you could cut it," he grumbled, setting his briefcase down. He glanced over at the desk. "You look goddam cheerful."

Drops of water clung to his battered hat, his thick graying hair, and shapeless jacket. He smelled faintly of stale cigarettes, though Ginny hadn't noticed him smoking the day before. His eyes, peering out from a nest of wrinkles, looked sour and skeptical.

She smiled. "Coffee?"

Frank glanced warily around the room. A coffeepot that had not been there yesterday perked slowly on the counter. "Yeah, sounds good. Thanks," he added awkwardly.

Ginny filled two mugs she had brought from home, handed him the one with the stripes, and kept the one with the cat for herself. "There's sugar in that box."

Frank gave her a quick glance. "Observant, aren't you?" he murmured. Yesterday when he had brought them both coffee from the business office, she had noticed two packets of sugar. She watched him take a sip.

"Good coffee," he said appreciatively. "Have you found someone to mind your little girl?"

Ginny stiffened. "I can stay as late as you need me."

Frank set his cup down with the look of someone determined to get things straight. "Look, I'm just an inconsiderate slob whose wife always took care of the kids."

"You're not inconsiderate." Her words were automatic, but as she spoke she realized they were true. This was the man who had hiked down Jackson Ridge with a blanket and a flask of whiskey just for her.

"The coffee's good," Frank said, "but you don't have to butter me up."

"Look, Frank, I thought about it last night, and I realized a job like this can't be done on a regular schedule. And yes, I did find someone to look after Rebecca."

"Rebecca. How old is she?"

"Nine."

"You're on your own, too, aren't you? Husband dead?"

Ginny nodded.

"Tough raising a kid alone."

"Do you have children?" she asked, taking a grudging interest in him.

"Two girls. Grown now, married. Their mother and I split up a couple of years ago."

Before she could think of a reply, Craig Wheeler stuck his head into Dispatch. "Carver in? Oh, there you are. Got a minute?"

"Lots of them. Come on in."

Craig glanced uneasily down the hall. "How about my office?"

Frank and Ginny followed him through the station to the Silviculture Department. The main room was deserted, the crew already gone. Craig led them to his desk and pulled up a couple of chairs.

"I've been thinking about what you said, about someone disliking Nino." He glanced through the open door at the far end of the room and lowered his voice. "God, I hate this."

Frank's face remained impassive. He's heard it all before, Ginny thought. Craig looked like a kid whose conscience was forcing him to snitch. But wasn't that what Frank wanted her to do? She sat up straight, remembering his words. We're going to be talking to a lot of people, people you know and I don't. I'm going to want your opinions on them. People at the district, in Galina—she knew almost everyone in the valley.

"Maybe Ginny's already told you, though," Craig said.

She gave him a startled look.

"About Len. I think everyone liked Nino, except Len Whittaker."

As soon as he said it, she knew it was true. She nodded slowly. The fuss Len had made about issuing Nino a red card, saying he shouldn't go on fires because he hadn't been to fire school. This from Len, who privately considered training a waste of time. She had seen him, more than once, pass Nino in the hall without a word, as though he weren't there.

"What makes you think Whittaker disliked him?" Frank asked.

"Well, he didn't want me to hire him."

"Did he say that?" The words were out of Ginny's mouth before she could stop them. She glanced at Frank, who gave her a slight nod. It was all right, then.

"He asked if I'd considered Nino's record. I'd talked to Harriet already, and I told him so. After all, Harriet knew him a lot better than Len." Craig shrugged. "What got me thinking about it, though, was something Sarah said."

He turned to Frank. "Sarah's my wife. We had dinner at Holiday Acres a couple weeks ago, and somehow Nino's name came up. I didn't notice anything, myself, but on the way home Sarah said it was like a ghost had sat down at the table. Like they'd all agreed not to talk about him."

Frank leaned forward, suddenly alert. "When was this?"

"I've got it written down." Craig fished a datebook out of his pocket. "Here, November twenty-second. Saturday evening. They ask us over a couple times a year."

"Who mentioned Alvarez?"

"I don't remember."

"Take a minute and think. Who was there?"

"Well, Harriet and Len, of course, Danny, Susie, Magda and Joe Gilmore, Sarah and me."

"What did you talk about during dinner?"

"Nothing important. We try not to talk shop, but you know how it is. I guess they'd just finished putting in some drainage ditches—then Magda and Susie talked about Polish cooking." Craig shrugged. "Nothing important."

"What were you talking about just before Alvarez's name came up?"

Craig frowned. "I can't remember. Just this big, awkward silence."

"Can you hear someone saying his name—Alvarez?"

Craig shook his head. "I'm sorry. Just the pause. Then Harriet said something, and everybody started talking all at once."

"OK. Thanks. Be sure to tell me if you remember."

Craig nodded. "I found some more of Nino's stuff, by the way—he left a backpack in one of the rigs. What should I do with it?"

Frank had come out to Galina during his first investigation, talked to Craig, and gone through the drawers in Alvarez's desk. He had not thought of searching the Forest Service trucks. "Have you looked at it yet?"

"No, when I saw whose it was I didn't touch it."

Frank got up. "OK. Let's go take a look."

NINO ALVAREZ had not left much behind. The pack held an extra pair of socks, a canteen, and a few odds and ends. Frank had these spread across the top of his desk and was going through them while Ginny took notes.

"One mechanical pencil, three grease pencils."

Craig nodded. "Most of this is Forest Service stuff."

"One compass." Frank picked up a small silver item for a closer look. "One St. Christopher's medal, not government issue." He put it next to the socks. Alvarez's personal items would be returned to his family.

All that remained were a few crumpled balls of paper. He smoothed out the first to reveal a column of numbers. "Is this his handwriting?"

Craig studied it for a moment. "Yeah. Figuring out his overtime."

Next came a telephone memo, a printed form with blanks for the message. Harriet Whittaker's name was penciled in, along with the date, Friday, October thirty-first.

"Well, well." Frank considered the memo. Things were starting to point. Everyone's life was an organized whole, no matter how scattered it might look at first glance. There was the need to make a living, family, home, hobbies—always some central point. In Alvarez's case, it looked as though that point might be Holiday Acres.

"I guess we'd better give Mrs. Whittaker a call."

"She's not home," Ginny said, looking at the memo. "I talked to Len this morning, and he said she wouldn't be back until eleven. But that's Maureen Evans's handwriting."

MAUREEN EVANS was a tall, sulky-looking blonde. She brought a whiff of scent with her into the little office. Frank guessed she was in her early thirties, then exercised a policeman's prerogative by asking her. Thirty-six.

They went through a few preliminary questions before he showed her the telephone memo. "Did you take this?"

She gave it an indifferent glance. "It's my handwriting."

"Do you remember the call?"

"I take a lot of calls."

"How about this one?"

She sighed and looked at the date. "Harriet called and asked for Nino. He wasn't in, so I took the message."

"She didn't mention what she wanted?"

"No."

"Thank you," he said with exaggerated politeness. "Now, were you at the Galina tavern that same day, October thirty-first?"

"I might have been. I go there sometimes."

Frank glanced at the papers in front of him. "Some other Forest Service employees were there that evening—Ken Rasmussen, Eric Browning, and Scott Pritchard. It was Halloween."

"I remember. Eric bought me a beer."

"Does he do that often?"

Maureen's gaze was level. "I'm not sure that's any of your business."

Frank smiled to himself and let it pass. "You spoke to Nino Alvarez, also."

"I might have, if he was there."

"He was. What did you say to him?"

Once again Maureen's eyes met his. "It was just about some phone calls."

"Yes?" Had she hesitated just a moment? Frank thought she had.

"The same guy kept calling. Some contractor. I wanted to make sure Nino was getting the messages."

Somehow Frank could not picture Maureen Evans putting in even an extra minute on her job, especially not when someone was buying her a drink. "And was he?"

She shrugged. "I guess so."

"You didn't mention the call from Harriet Whittaker?"

"No."

"Do you know what Alvarez planned to do after leaving the tavern?"

"Go home, I guess. Isn't that what he always did on weekends?"

"Did you see him leave?"

Maureen thought for a moment. "Yeah, I did."

"When was that?" Frank prompted.

"I don't know exactly, but it was starting to get crowded. Maybe around six, six thirty."

"Was he alone?"

"I didn't see anyone go with him."

Frank asked a few more questions, trying to pin down the contractor's name and the times of his calls, though he frankly doubted the man's existence. When Maureen finally left, after promising to look for the phone messages, she gave no sign of realizing that she might have been the last person—next to the killer—to speak with Alvarez.

Ginny fanned her notebook, clearing out Maureen's perfume.

Frank chuckled. "I'll bet she keeps the boys around here hopping."

"Poor Eric Browning's been tagging after her for almost a year."

"Is she married?"

"Divorced. She has two girls in middle school. Wild, from what I hear. They spend a lot of time with their father in California."

"Boyfriend?"

"No." Ginny gave him a curious look. "She goes out a lot, but no one steady. That's kind of funny, isn't it?"

"Maybe she likes to play the field."

AT ELEVEN Ginny called Holiday Acres and arranged for them to meet Harriet there at noon. A thick, muffling fog still lay over the Neskanie Valley. Curtains of clammy mist eddied across the river and banked up along the highway. Frank and Ginny peered through the windshield as their truck crept along at twenty miles an hour. Frank flipped the headlights from dim to bright and back again without making any appreciable change in visibility. Specks of color appeared in the mist ahead of them, blinked, reappeared, and then a loaded log truck roared past, running lights blazing red and yellow in the fog.

Frank slowed down even more. A sign materialized ahead of them, pointing to the Tenmile River bridge. "Is this where we turn?"

"This is it." Ginny's own house was on the same road, five point six miles from the bridge, on the right just past the third sharp bend.

Across the bridge they came upon a truck loaded with Christmas trees. The driver was outside cranking down on the bindings that held the bundled firs in place. A little farther on they passed another load, and then they made out the big red-and-green Holiday Acres sign. Behind it thousands of perfectly shaped Christmas trees marched off into the fog. A crew was busy nearby, loading a flatbed truck.

"Looks like a big operation," Frank said.

"It is."

"And Harriet Whittaker's been running it since her first husband died?"

Ginny nodded. "I don't think there's anything she hasn't done—shearing trees, running a chain saw, driving the tractor, plus books and dealing with the buyers, too."

"She's married to Len Whittaker now, isn't she? Does he help out?"

"Oh, yes. He figures on taking early retirement next summer. Then he and Harriet can run the place full-time."

Frank drove slowly up the long driveway, avoiding the worst of the bumps. The fog thinned near the top of the hill, and as they neared the packing shed a helicopter came into view, approaching from the fields with a sling of Christmas trees dangling from its belly. Frank parked the truck, and they got out. The helicopter came closer, the *whup-whup-whup* of the blades growing louder.

Ginny shaded her eyes against the pale winter sun and peered up at the ship. "I'll bet that's Ducks Wilson. And there's Len, guiding him in."

Len Whittaker stood a few hundred yards away, across the road on a small rise that gave a view of both the fields and the sheds near the house. He was wearing rain gear and a hard hat and talking into a hand-held radio, his attention focused on the helicopter that was now hovering beside the packing shed. Following his instructions, Ducks lowered the ship until the load of trees bumped gently on the ground. Two men unhooked the sling and dragged the trees toward the shed. The helicopter rose, banked, and headed back to the fields for another load.

A crew of women was busy in the packing shed, sorting and tagging trees for shipment. Everyone wore heavy rain gear, the shiny rubber slicked over with mud. Two women stood beside the roaring motor of a baler, feeding trees in. The machine wrapped them up with a whoosh of cord, then spat them out again. The rest of the crew chattered away in spite of the noise.

Ginny waved to the packing crew. They were all from Galina, all glad to get out of the house for a few weeks to make a little money for Christmas. They smiled back, their faces smudged with dirt. Their hands never stopped moving trees. The sharp, clean scent of the firs hung over everything, making Ginny's nose tingle in spite of the damp.

Magda Gilmore came out of the shed and hurried up to them. "Hello, hello, Ginny," she said, in her faint Polish accent. "We've all heard the news. This must be the policeman, yes?" She cocked her head at Frank.

Ginny introduced them.

"He looks like a policeman," Magda said. "The gossip we hear is that Nino was murdered."

"That's how it looks," Frank said. "You knew Mr. Alvarez?"

"Knew him? Of course I knew him. We worked like this." She held up two fingers, close together. "During the harvest I ran the packing shed, he ran the field crew. In the summer we sheared trees together. And I never called him Mr. Alvarez."

"Did you like him?"

Her weathered face softened in a smile. "Impossible not to like him. A sweet boy." She turned to Ginny. "What is this we hear, also, that Nino had a wife, that he had children?"

Ginny glanced at Frank, who gave her a slight nod.

"Apparently he did, Magda. Two young daughters."

"He told no one, no one here." She shook her head sadly. "The poor babies."

Frank waited a moment to show his sympathy with the Alvarez children, then moved on to the question that had occurred to him as soon as he had heard Magda's name. "You had dinner at the Whittakers' a couple of weeks ago, didn't you?"

Magda thought for a moment, then looked up. "Yes, we did, my husband and I."

"The Wheelers were there, too."

She nodded. "Craig and Sarah. Very nice people."

"Alvarez's name came up in the conversation."

"Yes." Her eyes flashed. "It made an awkwardness. That was before we knew he was dead, of course."

"Who brought it up?"

"Danny. He did it on purpose, to make someone mad, I think, or to hurt someone. Danny is not a nice boy."

The baling machine clattered, spat, and came to a stop. In the sudden quiet they heard the helicopter again, the distant *whup-whup-whup* of the rotor blades echoing off the hills.

"Harriet's expecting you," Magda said abruptly, nodding in the direction of the house. "In her office." She turned away and went back to the packing shed.

SIX

SOMEONE WAS WATCHING. Frank felt it as they walked up the path to a big split-level house that would have looked more comfortable on a suburban lot. In a suburb, though, it would have been landscaped with azaleas and showy rhododendrons; here its foundations lay bare behind a straggle of grass. The windows, curtains opened, stared blankly at the sky, but behind at least one of them somebody followed their steps up to the door marked Holiday Acres Office. Frank knocked.

Harriet Whittaker took a minute to answer, though he suspected she had been standing right there, waiting. Without a word she led them down a short hallway and into her office. She closed the door.

"You must be Frank Carver," she said, shaking hands. "Len told me—I know you're here to ask about Nino. Won't you sit down? There's coffee, Ginny, if Mr. Carver would like some."

Ginny turned to the coffeepot, her face expressionless. Frank gave an inward shudder. This woman was acting too much like his former wife for comfort. She even looked a bit like Minerva; a chunky, big-boned woman neatly dressed in jeans, a ruffled shirt, and a Fair Isle cardigan. He had expected the working owner of a tree farm to look more like Magda Gilmore, with her craggy face and mud-spattered clothes. Harriet had skin like faded rose petals. Her short hair was neatly curled.

He gave Ginny a sheepish smile as he took his cup, then sipped politely while she got her notebook out and sat down. Harriet made small talk, not avoiding the subject at hand so much as waiting for him to bring it up.

"Nino Alvarez worked for you for a long time, didn't he?"

Harriet set her cup down. "Seven years. Wesley hired him before he died."

"And you kept him on?"

"Oh, yes. Nino was a fine employee."

She sat calmly waiting for his next question. She would answer that, too, and any others he cared to ask, but she was not going to give anything away. Frank guessed she probably expected him to ask why she had fired such a fine employee. So instead he went to something that had puzzled him all along.

"Why do you think Alvarez hid the fact that he had a family?"

Her eyes turned cautious. "I wouldn't say he hid it, exactly. He just never mentioned it."

"During the seven years he worked for you he got married and fathered two children. It's hard to believe he never mentioned any of that."

"He never said anything to me."

"Could we look at his W-4's?"

Ginny looked up, puzzled by the sudden change of subject. Surely Harriet knew more than she was telling. Why wasn't Frank going after it?

Harriet went to a row of file cabinets along the wall, took out a folder, and handed it to Frank. He rummaged through the papers until he found what he wanted.

"Here it is for last year, and he claimed only the one exemption. I'd call that hiding. No one passes up three tax exemptions without a reason."

Harriet remained silent. Frank closed the file and set it down. "Mrs. Whittaker, why did you call Alvarez on October thirty-first?"

She looked surprised for an instant, but unperturbed. "To make an appointment for that evening. He never showed up."

"What did you want to see him about?"

"It had to do with his job."

"The job he used to have."

"Yes."

"Why did he leave?"

"We had to let him go."

Like pulling teeth, and she could probably go on all afternoon. Frank leaned forward. "Mrs. Whittaker, I don't know why you fired Alvarez. No one I've talked to seems to know. But a man doesn't lose a job he's held for seven years without talking to someone, and pretty soon I'm going to find that someone. It will be easier if you just tell me."

"It doesn't have anything to do with—the way he died."

"How can you know that? Alvarez disappeared, and quite probably died, about the time of his appointment with you."

"Oh." Harriet fingered a button on her sweater. "All right. I intended to offer him his job back."

"Did he know that?"

"No. He didn't know why I wanted to talk to him."

"Why did you want him back?"

"Because he hadn't—" She stopped and tried again. "I had learned that he hadn't done the thing I'd fired him for."

"Which was?"

She glared at him.

"I will find out, Mrs. Whittaker."

"Embezzlement," she said sourly.

Frank's respect for her went up. She had side-stepped the word *murder*, but this one she pronounced without a twitch. "From your business? How much?"

"I'm not sure. At least ten thousand dollars."

"You've found the real culprit, then?"

Harriet's lips tightened. "I've learned that Nino didn't do it." She relaxed, just a little. "Mr. Carver, Nino was a good employee. A hard worker, responsible, never a complaint. I could hardly believe it when Len...when we discovered the money was missing. So you can imagine how I felt when I learned he hadn't done it. I called the station and left a message. He called me back later that afternoon and agreed to stop by on his way to Harmony. I wanted him back. I was even ready to make up the wages he'd lost."

"What did you think when he didn't turn up?"

"I guessed he'd changed his mind about seeing me. He had a lot of pride, you know." She glanced at Ginny, then back to Frank. "I don't want everyone in Galina talking about that ten thousand dollars."

"Do you want to report it? Embezzlement is a crime."

"No. I don't want it public."

Frank nodded. "Your choice. I'll warn you, though, that if it's connected to Alvarez's death, it will come out." He stood up. "We'll have a look around the farm now, and then we can leave you in peace."

Ginny hastily closed her notebook, surprised for the second time that morning. Why wasn't Frank asking more questions? Anyone could see that Harriet was holding something back.

"I don't have much time to give you a tour," Harriet grumbled.

"That's all right, Mrs. Whittaker." Frank kept his voice polite, as though this was a social occasion. "We can manage by ourselves."

She stood in the doorway as they left, clearly reluctant to let them go alone. When they were out of earshot, Frank stopped to look around. The rambling house was set on top of a small hill, with the equipment and packing sheds off to one side. The fog had settled back in again; it swirled slowly around them, giving glimpses of the fields with their lines of neatly trimmed trees. The helicopter was out of sight, perhaps grounded by the weather. In the packing shed, the baling machine roared away, spitting out bundled trees.

"Now there's a woman with something to hide," Frank said.

"At least she told you why she fired Nino." Ginny zipped her jacket up, tucked her hands under her arms, and shivered.

"That, I think, was the truth. She doesn't really tell lies, did you notice? She just doesn't answer the question."

She gave him an appreciative glance. "I *have* noticed. Why didn't you push her?"

"Not ready yet. And sometimes you can learn just as much without playing hardball."

Ginny considered this. "You ask Harriet a question, and she says something that sounds like an answer. Only it isn't."

"She did it three times, once about Alvarez's family and twice about why she fired him."

"So whatever she's hiding has to do with Nino."

"Or with her husband. Len Whittaker is obviously the one who wanted to sack Alvarez."

"That would fit in with what Craig said, about Len not liking him. But maybe that's *why* he didn't like Nino, because he thought he took the money."

"Could be." Frank paused. "Who's your first choice for embezzling ten thousand dollars?"

"Oh, that's easy." She stopped.

"Yes?"

"I don't know that I have a choice," she said lamely.

He waited, watching her. Ginny did not meet his eyes. Tiny drops of moisture clung to her thick, curly hair and dark eyebrows, blurring the lines of her face so that she seemed very far away. He remembered that she was a widow, and wondered which was worse, having marriage snatched away from you, or ruining it through your own faults. It occurred to him that she must get pretty lonely.

Sympathy, even empathy, were part of his job. He had to know, really know, what other people felt in order to figure out what they might have done. But sympathy was not going to help here.

"These people are friends of yours, aren't they?" he asked.

Ginny nodded.

"Look, Mrs. Trask, if you're working with me, you're going to have to spill it. Sooner or later, everything you know about them. If you're not working for me, tell me so." He paused. "Tell me soon."

"OK."

Had he made a mistake in taking her on? Once Hunsaker had saddled him with an assistant, perhaps he should have insisted on someone with professional training. If Ginny backed out now, he would try to get Deputy Wilcox, or maybe someone from another district.

"Let's get going, then. I want to see where Nino stayed when he worked here."

They got into the truck. Ginny directed him past a patch of fir trees, then down a small hill. Frank eased the truck along the rutted road, giving her time to think. She was too absorbed to notice his silence. What *did* she think about Harriet and her family? Were they really friends? Harriet appeared to like her, but treated her as though she were a rather stupid child. With Len she had the half-joking, can-do relationship the Forest Service encouraged between boss and employee. He got on her nerves after a while—his comments about women were a little hard to take—but as bosses went he wasn't bad. And Danny—she shied away from thinking too much about Danny. That left Susie, and there she came to a big stop. Susie was the only one of the bunch she genuinely liked.

"Is this the place?" Frank pulled over and shut the motor off. The little wooden house, weathered to a gray that made it seem almost a thickening of the fog, was the oldest he had yet seen in Galina. The front door and two windows looked out through a sagging porch. A few leafless shrubs grew near the steps. The roof was new, though, the glass in the windows unbroken, and the place had a tidy air in spite of being run-down.

They got out of the truck. "Susie thinks this is the original homestead," Ginny said, relieved to be talking about things for a moment, instead of people. "It looks old enough."

"Did the Meissner family settle this piece?"

"No, Wes and Harriet bought it when they got married. Wes was from Washington—Kelso, I think. Harriet grew up right down the road, though, in my house. She holds my mortgage."

Frank lifted his eyebrows. "Is that why you got the coffee?"

She looked up. So he *had* noticed. "It's just easier not to argue." She stopped. This was not what Frank wanted from her. "Harriet's been giving orders for so long I don't think she realizes how she sounds anymore."

Frank stepped up on the porch and tried the door. It swung slowly inward to reveal a large room almost filled by two big tables. A wood stove stood in one corner, under a bare light bulb. Tools, rolls of plastic, and canvas tarps filled the shelves along the back wall.

"Looks like they're using it for storage," Frank said.

They went inside, their steps sounding hollow on the wood floor. The house smelled musty. Twigs and bits of litter lay in drifts beneath the tables. Ginny peered into the tiny kitchen tacked onto the back, empty except for the sink and an unplugged refrigerator. Perhaps Nino had done his cooking on the wood stove. Back in the main room Frank was standing with his hands on his hips, turning in a slow circle, apparently studying the walls.

"Alvarez lived here?" he asked.

"Except for weekends, from what I understand."

"He followed the same pattern with the Forest Service, didn't he? Lived there during the week, drove home to his family on the weekends."

Ginny nodded.

"I wonder if he died here."

"What makes you think that?"

"Just a hunch. Look at all those rolls of plastic. And these." He went to the far wall and carefully took down a long knife shaped like a machete or a broadsword. He ran a finger along the blade. "Perfect for killing someone. What do they do with these, anyway? There must be fifty of them up here."

"They're shearing knives," Ginny said. She took the knife from him, hefted it, and tried a few strokes through the air. "They trim the trees every summer, to make them grow bushy. I've seen Harriet work with two of these things, one in each hand."

"Harriet," Frank murmured, gazing at the blade.

"We don't know for sure how Nino was killed. Could it have been a shearing knife?"

"You saw the autopsy report. Jarvis says the cause of death was possibly a blow to the skull, possibly with a sharp instrument. The body was too mutilated to tell. Well, you saw that, too."

"Yes." She hung the knife back up on the wall.

"Those must be pretty dangerous to work with."

"They are, though I don't think there's ever been a serious injury at Holiday Acres." She took a pair of protective chaps down from a shelf. A few twigs spilled out as she showed him the thick pads crisscrossed with little cuts.

They were silent for a moment. Ginny scuffed her foot through the debris under the table. "Looks like they just chucked everything in here after Nino left." She bent down to pick up a small branch. The needles were still green, the bud tightly furled at one end and the other neatly clipped. Dozens of them lay on the floor, probably brought in with the shearers' chaps and heavy gloves.

They both looked up as a truck came to a stop outside. A door slammed, and they heard Len's voice.

"Frank? Ginny?" He poked his head through the doorway.

"Hi, Len," Ginny said brightly. She could not get over the feeling that they were trespassing.

"Harriet said you were looking around." Len stepped inside, peered for a moment, and flipped the wall switch. A harsh glare filled the room. "Thought I'd see if you needed anything."

Frank nodded. "Mostly I want to find out more about Alvarez. I guess you knew him pretty well?"

"He worked here," Len said. "We weren't pals."

"Must not have been, if you got him fired."

Len looked at Frank for a moment, then chuckled. "Mind if I sit down?" He upended a wooden crate and sat on it. "Might as well get comfortable while you grill me."

Frank pulled up another crate. He had planned to question Whittaker next, and though he would have preferred a more formal setting, he was willing to take advantage of the moment. He had planned to start with general questions, the way he had with Harriet, but something about Len irritated him—perhaps just the man's self-assurance—and he was not sorry that he had plunged right in. He glanced at Ginny, perched on a corner of the table with her notebook out, and plunged in deeper.

"What made you suspect embezzlement?"

"There was a whole slug of money missing." Len planted his hands on his knees and explained. "After Harriet and I got married, I went through the books. I went through everything, the way you do when you're taking on a new operation. Early in the summer I got the feeling something was wrong. Our labor costs were way too high."

"Who was doing the bookkeeping?" Had Harriet sent her husband to keep an eye on them? Frank suspected that not much happened at Holiday Acres without her permission.

"No one, really. Cindy Adams had been doing it, until she quit to have a baby. Danny was supposed to have taken over, but I couldn't see that he'd done much. Harriet was keeping the checkbook balanced. Other than that, it was a mess."

"What made you suspect Alvarez? From what I've heard of his job, it doesn't sound like he'd have access to large sums of money."

"He hired the field crews. Mexicans, a lot of them. Some of them weren't any nationality at all." Len chuckled at his joke.

"Meaning?"

"They didn't exist. We were paying people who didn't exist."

"That must of been tricky to pull off. Social security numbers, W-2's, FICA, all that stuff."

"He was contracting for whole crews, then drawing one check for the crew boss to cover everything. That way he avoided the payroll details. It was slick enough."

"Your wife says it wasn't him, though. She found out that Alvarez was innocent."

Len nodded. "I know that's what she thinks, but I still say he did it." He leaned forward. "You look at Harriet, you'd never think she's got a soft spot. She's plenty tough. But a woman can't run an operation like this by herself, not for years and years. She'd gotten to where she really depended on Alvarez. Depended on him too much. Now she just can't bring herself to admit she was wrong." He straightened up. "I'm not going to push the issue. The money's gone, Alvarez is dead. She might as well believe what she likes."

"You didn't care much for him, did you?"

"It's hard to like a thief."

"What did you think when Wheeler hired him on at Galina?"

"I thought he was making a mistake, and I told him so. After that I kept my mouth shut."

Frank nodded. They were quiet for a minute.

"Things going OK with Ginny?" Len asked. He gave her a wink. "I know you couldn't ask for a better worker."

"We're getting along," Frank said.

Ginny nodded. "How's Maureen doing with the radio?"

"Fine, just fine. We missed you yesterday, of course, but we're managing. Speaking of which, now Harriet's back I'd better be getting down to the station."

"It must keep you pretty busy, working two jobs," Frank said.

"It sure does. I suppose Ginny told you I'm taking early retirement next year."

"No, I hadn't heard that. Got any plans?"

Len nodded. "Yeah, I figure with better management we could increase our production fifty percent." He paused. "Frank, my wife and I would both appreciate it if this business about the money didn't get out. I know you have to check every little detail, but this doesn't have anything to do with Alvarez's death."

"Oh?" Frank looked up. "How would you know that, Mr. Whittaker?"

Len chuckled again. "I guess you got me there. Well, let me know if I can do anything for you. I'll be at the station the rest of the day." He and Frank both stood up. "By the way, I don't *mind* if you call me Len."

When the sound of his truck had faded in the distance, Frank and Ginny stepped out onto the porch. Frank reached back in to flip off the light switch and pull the door shut. He took a minute to stretch, giving his shoulders a good shake.

"What's Whittaker like to work for?"

Ginny shrugged. "He's OK."

"How long have they been married?"

"Not quite a year. They had the wedding in the big house, after Christmas. It was a major event."

"Is Len a full partner in Holiday Acres?"

"Sounds like it, doesn't it?"

Frank nodded. "It does, indeed. Well, let's go back up to the house. I wouldn't mind talking to this Danny character." He glanced at Ginny. "What's so funny?"

"Calling Danny a character. You know, to me they're real people."

"Yeah, I know. That's part of the problem."

Harriet answered the door. Danny was gone, she told them in a tired voice, and Susie was asleep. "It's been a shock to her, this business about Nino. The doctor gave her some tranquilizers."

Frank lifted his eyebrows. "Tranquilizers."

"Yes, Mr. Carver. I might as well tell you, because you will find out anyway, that my daughter is mildly manic-depressive. Something like this can hit her pretty hard."

"Was she especially fond of Alvarez?"

"He was kind to her. Not many men are kind to Susie."

SEVEN

THEY STOPPED AT THE foot of the Holiday Acres' driveway, ready to pull out onto Tenmile Road. Frank waited for a white station wagon to go by.

"Frank," Ginny said. "That's Danny Meissner."

Frank hopped out of the truck and flagged the car down just as it pulled into the driveway. Danny lowered the window. He caught sight of Ginny, still sitting in the truck, and gave her a little wave.

"Hello, officer," Danny said. "Wasn't breaking the speed limit, was I?"

"Not that I could tell. You're Danny Meissner?"

"I'm afraid so." Danny's smile faded slowly. "You must be the new cop Len was talking about."

"I'd like to ask you a few questions, Mr. Meissner."

"Right here?"

"Would you prefer my office?"

Danny looked at him, then shook his head. "There's a parking area just off the driveway, past that big tree. Let's pull in there."

A few minutes later Danny leaned against the side of Frank's truck. Ginny spread her notebook on the hood. Frank opened with what she was coming to recognize as his usual questions, extracting from Danny a brief history of his relationship with the victim. He had known Alvarez for years, and during the time he was nominally managing Holiday Acres he had been his boss.

"How long were you the manager?"

"About two years, until Len moved in. Not that Harriet ever took her eyes off me."

"Do you think Alvarez was an embezzler?"

Danny's head jerked up. "You must have talked to the old lady already. I'm surprised she told you that."

"Do you think he did it?"

"Who else could it have been?"

Ginny looked up. Danny's face was open and guileless. It was an expression she had seen before.

"I don't know, Mr. Meissner," Frank replied. "Who else do you think it could have been?"

"Well," Danny said, hitching his elbows up on the hood of the truck, "except for the timing I'd pick my new stepfather. He would have had to start right in at it though, just as soon as they were married, and you'd think he'd wait a year or two before he started bilking his wife."

"I take it you don't care much for Len Whittaker."

"He's not my favorite person, no."

"Any special reason?"

"He's a martinet. You know what that means? Everything by the book. I looked it up—it's a good word. He's also tight with money."

Frank nodded. "What about Alvarez? Were the two of you friends?"

"We were. I liked Nino. He was a good dude. No matter what he might have done around here, he didn't deserve to die."

"Very few people do," Frank observed. "Did Alvarez have enemies?"

"I guess he must have, huh?"

Frank stopped and studied Danny for a moment. Lounging against the truck, he had been the picture of insolence. That pose had vanished as he made his declaration of loyalty to Alvarez, and now he seemed to have trouble recapturing it. Frank decided to give his fish a bit more line.

"I want to find out what happened to Alvarez. You were his friend. Do you want to know the truth?"

"I guess so."

"Is there some reason you *don't* want to? Or that you don't want me to find out?"

Danny looked up. "No, there's no reason."

"Like maybe that you took that money yourself?"

"What? What the hell! Is that an accusation?"

"It's a question."

Danny glared at him. "Listen, Agent Carver, sir, you can ask all the questions you want, but I don't have to answer them."

Ginny almost cringed as she listened to Danny. Why didn't he just shut up? Because that's the way he is, she told herself. An average kind of guy, a little young for his age, lost on a crashing sea of anger. Touch him in the wrong place and he lashes out, hurting, hostile—and there were so many wrong places.

Frank's response was mild. "No, you don't have to."

"Who says I took the money?"

"No one. I'm only asking. Now, did Alvarez have enemies?"

Danny looked somewhat mollified. "He might have. Sometimes, the way he talked . . . You know, Nino had a whole other life. He must have. Seven years working out here, never went to a party, never had a date, running back to Harmony every chance he got."

"He had a wife and children in Harmony."

"That's what I heard. Amazing! I'll bet he didn't let on because of Harriet."

"Harriet?" Frank asked.

"Yeah, she wouldn't have approved. She liked to think Nino was all hers." Danny chuckled. "I guess she was wrong, huh?"

"What did you mean, Mr. Meissner, about the way Alvarez talked?"

"Oh, I just got the feeling there was something more going on. More than his family, I mean."

"Like what? Any ideas?"

"I don't know. Something to do with Mexico. Drugs, maybe."

Frank's eyebrows went up. "Did Alvarez use drugs?"

"I don't think so. But he might have been involved. Moving stuff through, you know."

"Thanks for the tip." Frank waited a moment, watching Danny. Had the ten thousand dollars gone for cocaine? Galina was such a sleepy little town, you'd think nothing had changed since the fifties, but Frank had worked in narcotics long enough to know better. Pot, junk, coke, it could turn up anywhere. And you might as well be burning hundred-dollar bills, when you got involved in that stuff.

"OK," he said. "We're done. For now."

Danny pushed himself away from the truck, gave Ginny a curt nod, and climbed into his car. He pulled out of the parking area and turned up the driveway to Holiday Acres.

Frank looked at Ginny. "What do you think?"

"I think Danny hates his mother and loves her at the same time. That's hardly news, though. I've thought that for years."

"What do you think about drugs?"

Ginny sketched a few doodles in her notebook. Finally she looked up. "Danny was busted for growing pot about eight years ago. He was under eighteen, and the case never went to court. Harriet and Wes fixed it up somehow."

"Anything recent?"

"Not that I know of, but Danny wouldn't tell me. And it's anyone's guess what he's been up to in California."

Frank nodded. "OK. We can ask Sheriff Holt if he knows anything. And now I guess we'd better get busy."

They climbed into the truck. "What next?" Ginny asked.

"We're going to start from the other end."

"The other end?"

Frank pulled out onto Tenmile Road. "We've traced Alvarez from the ranger station to the tavern. We'll have to confirm Maureen's statement about when he left, but for now we can accept it. Alvarez walks out the door of the Galina tavern, headed somewhere, maybe to Holiday Acres, maybe to his home in Harmony, and disappears."

"Until his body turns up."

"The next known fact," Frank said. "That's the end we're going to start from now."

They drove out to the Neskanie highway and turned west, away from Galina, then took the Jackson turn-off. The fog thinned as the truck climbed through the hairpin curves winding up the side of the ridge. Dark, massive firs loomed over the road, their tops lost in whiteness. The fog took on a golden glow as they rounded the final turn. Big holes appeared, and suddenly they were climbing out of it, trailing streamers of mist. The sky arched overhead, pure and blue, without a cloud in sight.

Frank pulled over as soon as they reached the top. Below them a lake of milky white spread away toward the ocean, its placid surface dotted with dark, humped ridges. To the east the white peaks of the Cascades glinted in the sun. Light poured from the sky, drawing up tendrils of mist, turning drops of water into iridescent sparks.

Frank shut the engine off. "Wow."

Ginny sat in silence, taken by surprise, once again, at the beauty spread around her. You lived in a place, doing your job, going shopping, washing clothes, and pretty soon it felt ordinary, like any other place. Then somehow, for a few minutes, you found yourself smack in the middle of God's most glorious creation.

They drove down the ridge to the fork where Hobson Logging's watchman had parked his trailer. It was shut up now, the old man apparently sleeping in. A little farther on they caught a glimpse of the logging operation across the draw. The yarder tower stood like a great tree, its cables stringing down into the fog. A logger waved as they went by. Another mile down the road they found the flagging Ginny had tied to mark the way into the unit.

They took a break, watching the last streamers of mist melt away among the trees. The air was crisp and clear, reminding Ginny of her early married days, when she and Dale had lived in a Forest Service district in the mountains. She ate some crackers, thinking about her husband. Dale Trask had always given one hundred percent to his job, even when that meant twelve or sixteen hours a day for weeks at a time. The Forest Service expected it. From her first day at Dispatch, Ginny had felt that expectation in the background, a steady pressure for more than she was willing to give.

Before, though, it had always been time. Time away from Rebecca, time away from the house, the garden, her sketch pad. Frank was asking for something different. She guessed that her familiarity with Galina was the main reason she had been detailed as his assistant. She had not imagined, though, that the investigation would include her nearest neighbors.

They pulled their boots on and started down the hill. The fog was almost gone when they reached the creek. Frank sat down on a log and stared at his wet trouser legs.

"You need some rain gear," Ginny said.

He glanced at her olive drab rubber pants. "Does it come in different colors?"

"Day-Glo yellow. What are we doing, anyway?"

"Trying to figure out how Alvarez got here." He sat quietly, taking in his surroundings. They all looked so much alike, these hillsides. Same red dirt, green leaves, even the same damn brown birds hopping around. The hillside in Seattle had been part of a public park, but once you were hunkered down in the brush, away from the traffic noise, it was much the same. This body had been hidden, the one in Seattle had been left as a warning. That was the difference.

Last night, he had promised himself he wouldn't think about it. He should have known how little control he had over his memory.

"I guess you've seen a lot of bodies," Ginny said.

He jerked his head up, thinking for a moment that she had read his mind. She was looking thoughtfully into the brush; he followed her gaze to the spot where Alvarez's remains had been found.

"I've seen a few. It's always a shock, though, death by violence."

"I was wondering if you'd get used to it. Of course, they'd all be strangers. It's not like finding someone you know."

He studied her for a moment. "They aren't always strangers."

"Oh." She met his eyes, then looked away. "Was it someone you knew very well?"

"My partner's daughter."

"Oh, no. Frank, I'm sorry."

He shrugged. "It was no worse than this has been for you."

"Did you get whoever had done it?"

"In the end. In the end we got them. And then I retired."

She fell silent, warned by his abruptness. At least he'd had the satisfaction of getting the killers. Did she need that satisfaction? Did it matter to her that Nino's killer be brought to justice? She was starting to feel that it did.

Frank had lifted his head to survey the ridges hemming them in on both sides. The one they had hiked down was heavily timbered, laced with game trails that ran for a dozen yards and then vanished in the brush. The opposite hill was a stark pattern of red earth and charred, blackened slash. "Alvarez weighed, what, a hundred and thirty? He wasn't a big man."

She studied the ridge line. "You think someone carried him in?"

"A living man doesn't wrap himself in black plastic to take a walk."

"A person could pack a hundred and thirty pounds. That's about the weight of a dressed buck. Of course, you could pack a buck out in pieces."

"Doc Jarvis thinks the body was entire until the coyotes got to it. But he admits he didn't have enough to be certain." Frank thought for a moment. "That road we came in on, is it the only way in here?"

"No, you could do it just as easy by taking the other fork. Easier, because you'd be coming through that burned unit and wouldn't have to fight the brush."

"Do the two roads come out at the end of the ridge?"

"I don't think so." Ginny reached back and felt around in the map pocket of her cruiser's vest. She was still carrying most of the gear she had taken out to do the fuels survey two days ago. Only two days—now it felt like a different era. She pulled a map out and spread it across her knees. "See, they both dead-end."

"What's this?" Frank asked. "This little mark here?"

"Jackson Lookout. It used to be a fire spotter's tower. The Forest Service stopped using it about ten years ago—now all the spotting's done from airplanes."

"But the tower's still there?"

"An attractive nuisance. The local kids go there to drink." She smiled. "My house is at the foot of the ridge. Last Fourth of July we could hear them setting off firecrackers."

Frank studied the map again. "That watchman's trailer is here, where the road forks. So anyone coming down either way would go right past him."

"Casey Mullen. He's a nosy old goat. We're thinking Nino disappeared on Halloween night?"

"I am. You haven't told me yet if you're still working for me."

"Oh." Ginny looked down at her hands, then back up. "I guess I'm here for the duration."

Frank smiled. She really did have nice eyes. "Glad to have you on board."

"Glad to be on board." She paused, then gave a little sigh. "My first choice for embezzling ten thousand dollars is definitely Danny Meissner."

CASEY MULLEN had poked his head out the door at the sound of their truck and was waiting for them, his watery eyes squinting in the sun. A fringe of grizzled hair stuck out below his cap. He stepped down from the trailer as they got out of the truck.

"Figured you'd be by sooner or later. Have a seat." He gestured to a pair of battered lawn chairs. "Found yourselves a body, I hear."

Frank cautiously lowered himself into one of the chairs while Casey poked at the coals of a small fire. The chair held. Ginny introduced him.

"How long have you been camped out here?" Frank asked.

"Figured you'd want to know that." Casey lifted his chin to reveal a scrawny neck and scratched at it for a moment, lost in thought. "Moved up here October twentieth, when the boys started falling. Don't really need anyone to keep an eye on things until they move the big equipment in, but the old lady and I were fighting again."

"Do you get much traffic up here?"

Casey nodded. "Fair amount, especially during hunting season."

"We're interested in the time around Halloween. Say from October thirty-first, that was a Friday, to the next Monday. Do you remember seeing anyone up here on those days?"

Casey snorted. "About half Galina, as I recall." He scratched his neck again. "Halloween day was pretty quiet, just a couple of hunters in the morning. Arnie and Bob Thompson, I think it was. Then towards evening a carload of kids, heading for the old lookout."

"Did you recognize any of them?"

"Oh, I know them. The Langendorf boy and that friend of his from the coast. The two Evans girls. Marty Geller's youngest—I forget his name right now. They went roaring down the road, then came roaring back about a half hour later."

"You didn't see anyone else in the car?"

"I didn't *see* anyone at all. It was dark. But I know who they were."

Frank smiled. "You said half Galina. Who else was up here?"

"Susie Meissner, in that little VW bug. That was about, oh, eight thirty, nine. Been dark for a while. She hadn't no sooner gone past than her mother came roaring down after her.''

Frank looked up. "Mrs. Whittaker?"

"That's right, Wes Meissner's widow."

"You're sure it was her?"

"Of course I'm sure." Casey glared at him. "What do you think they pay me for? Harriet Whittaker, in the Holiday Acres station wagon. They were down there maybe an hour. They left with Harriet following Susie, right on her tail. And no sooner were they gone than that passel of kids came through again. After that it was a free-for-all. Must have been ten, fifteen kids out at the old lookout. They didn't go home till two in the morning."

"Did you wait up for them?"

Casey gave the fire a truculent poke. "They let me know they was going, the little punks. Banged on the trailer."

"Sounds like you had a busy night."

Frank waited to see if Casey had anything else to say, but the old man appeared to have finished. He got up from his chair. "Well, thanks for your help. You can reach me at the ranger station if you think of anything else."

Casey raised his eyebrows. "Don't you want to hear about Danny Meissner?"

Frank abruptly sat back down. "Tell me."

"He was up here, too, the next morning. All decked out, he was. Camera, binoculars, shiny new boots. Must have sounded like a department store going through the brush.'' Casey rocked back on his heels with a little cackle of laughter.

''What was he doing?'' Frank asked.

''Hell, I don't know. Getting away from his mother, most likely.''

EIGHT

FRANK KEPT HIS EYES on the road as they entered the
steep turns looping back down to the highway. The
smell of coffee reached his nose. He turned to glance
at Ginny. She had a cup balanced in one hand as she
poured, letting her thermos sway with the bumping of
the truck.

Frank sniffed appreciatively. "And here I thought
we'd have to drive all the way into Galina for coffee."

Ginny snapped the cap back on the thermos.
"Haven't offered you any yet."

Frank blinked. Was she smiling? Yes, just a little.
Trying not to. The game would be to get the coffee
without actually asking for it. He let his face sag into
the pathetic look he used with his grandchildren.

"Oh, my God," said Ginny, "you look like a
bloodhound. Give me your cup."

Frank was still chuckling as he took the first sip. He
gave a little sigh and then got down to business.
"Who've we talked to so far?"

Ginny flipped her notebook open. "Just today? Or
yesterday too?"

"The works."

"Yesterday was Craig Wheeler, then Rosie Loomis at the tavern. This morning Craig again, then Maureen—"

"About the telephone calls."

Ginny nodded. "Then Harriet, Len, Danny—"

"Who doesn't like his stepfather."

"—and Casey Mullen."

Frank thought for a moment. "According to Casey, almost everyone at Holiday Acres was up here on Jackson Ridge sometime during that Halloween weekend."

Ginny scanned her notes. "Everyone except Len."

"Any of the others, though, had a chance to dump the body down in that draw."

"There were all those kids, too."

"True, but none of them had a connection. Not that we know of, anyway."

Ginny nodded. "We haven't talked to Susie."

"Her mother doesn't want us to, either. What's this business about her being manic-depressive? And where do you think they were this morning?"

Ginny shrugged. "A couple of years ago Susie was seeing a psychologist in Longmont. Maybe that's where they went."

Frank grunted. "There's something going on at that place. Ten thousand dollars missing, Whittaker acting like he's running things, when according to everyone else Harriet's in charge. Harriet claims she didn't even know Alvarez had a family. And now Danny's ready to accuse Whittaker of anything."

"He didn't accuse him of murder," Ginny said.

"That's true, and I'd guess that he would have, if he'd had any grounds for it." Frank swirled the last of the coffee around in his cup. "Quite a bunch, aren't they?"

BACK AT THE STATION, Ginny started in on her notes while Frank worked on the daily report. At five she called home to tell Alice she would be late and learned that Rebecca had gotten into a fight at school. With her research project well underway, Rebecca considered herself the local authority on Bigfoot. She had felt compelled to defend the creature's reputation for gentleness against two fifth-graders who had loudly accused him of killing Nino Alvarez.

"Did it come to blows?" Ginny asked, apprehensive.

"No, a teacher broke it up."

"Good. Alice, I'm so glad you're here."

Finally she called Holiday Acres and arranged with Harriet to go out there the next afternoon.

"She wants Susie to sleep in," she told Frank.

"That's OK. We'll be busy in the morning."

"With what?"

"We're going to Harmony. I want to see Alvarez's family again."

"What's her name?" Ginny asked. "Nino's wife."

"Felicia."

"How old is she?"

"Early twenties." He paused. "I'd like you to talk to Felicia Alvarez alone, if you get the chance."

"What do I talk to her about?"

"Anything will do. There's something about her I just don't get."

HARMONY WAS ONE of the oldest settlements in Oregon. It had spread slowly beside a bend of the Willamette River, a town of straight, tree-lined streets heavy with shade through the long summer afternoons. Now, in early December, with rain falling and not a pedestrian in sight, it looked forlorn and abandoned.

Frank drove down the main street, past Victorian brick storefronts decorated for Christmas, beneath street banners in Spanish and English. At the edge of the town they passed a school just as the bell rang for recess. Kids spilled out onto the playground, ignoring the rain. At least half of them were Mexican-Americans, with dark skin, black hair, and sparkling brown eyes.

They followed the road out of town for another mile, past a low hill, then took a couple of turns and pulled into a driveway. Ginny sat up with a little yawn. She had gotten home after ten the night before, and had dozed off more than once during the long drive. She peered through the rain-streaked window at Nino's home.

It could have been any suburban house, three bedrooms tucked into a single story with a double garage converted into an extra room. Low shrubs hid the foundation, and the tidy lawn was edged with bricks. A line of poplars grew down one side of the property; on the other stretched a waterlogged field. Two more houses stood across the road. The Alvarez family had very few neighbors.

"Looks like they're home," Frank said, glancing at the station wagon and the battered pickup in the driveway. He opened his door; in the distance a tractor muttered softly. A curtain twitched in the living-room window. "Looks like they know we're here."

They hurried to the shelter of the narrow front porch. Frank rang the bell once, waited, then rang again. Finally, on the third ring, the door opened just a crack to show a pair of anxious brown eyes.

"Yes?" asked the young woman.

"Mrs. Alvarez, I'm Frank Carver, the officer who's investigating your husband's death. I came out and spoke with you about a month ago, when he was first missing."

The woman was watching his mouth, nodding slightly with the rhythm of his words. He stopped. "Mrs. Alvarez, do you remember me?"

"Yes?" she asked again. Suddenly she closed the door.

"Damn it," Frank muttered. He rapped sharply on the door and waited. Finally it opened again. This time they were facing a short, stocky man of about thirty-five.

He glared at them suspiciously. "What do you want?"

"I'm Frank Carver, Mr. Alvarez, the officer investigating your brother's death. I was here about a month ago."

"I remember," the man said.

"I need to ask you and your brother and Mrs. Alvarez some more questions. May we come in?"

The man grudgingly admitted them. He led them through the living room, his muddy boots scuffing across the carpet, and into the dining area. Two little girls stared from the kitchen door. The older girl, who could not have been more than four, wore braids that hung almost to her waist. The younger one had her finger in her mouth.

Felicia shooed her daughters into the kitchen. Ginny stepped forward. Should she follow them, talk to them now? But no, Frank was introducing her to the man, whose name was Eduardo.

He glanced at her, making no attempt to take her outstretched hand. "You're a cop, too?"

"I'm here to take notes." She stared back at him, wishing for the first time that she had a definite status. At least then she would have a snappy answer to that question.

"Mrs. Trask is my deputy," Frank said. She could have hugged him. "Is Luis around?"

"He's in the field," Eduardo said. "Sit down. Felicia will bring coffee."

When they were seated Eduardo pulled his boots off and set them neatly on a piece of newspaper beside the glass doors that looked out on the backyard. Ginny got her notebook out, wondering how she was going to take notes in Spanish. Eduardo's English seemed fine, but Nino's wife—widow—didn't appear to have understood anything Frank had said. What did he expect her to do if she ever did get Felicia alone?

She looked up again, and finally took in the scene through the glass doors. Beyond the back lawn stretched a field of little firs that could have come straight from Holiday Acres. A tractor chugged up the road between the field and the poplars, hauling a trailer piled high with bundled Christmas trees.

"Here comes Luis now," said Eduardo. The tractor sputtered to a stop beside a shed. Luis climbed down, took off his boots and rain gear, and came in through the glass doors. As he sat down Felicia Alvarez brought in a tray with coffee, sugar, cups and saucers and set it on the table. She started back to the kitchen.

"Felicia," Eduardo said softly. "*Queda te.*"

She sat down. Eduardo poured coffee. Ginny stole a glance at Felicia. Her thick black hair was wrapped into a knot at the back of her neck, her downcast eyes hidden by heavy lashes.

Frank had already decided not to question them separately. They had had plenty of time to agree on a story, he'd told Ginny on the way out, if that was what they had in mind. He thought, too, from his earlier visit, that he might need an interpreter with Felicia. His Spanish was good enough to pick up the gist of what was said, but he could not conduct a thorough questioning.

"How is Mrs. Alvarez's mother?" he asked. "Is she at home?"

"She's resting with the children," Eduardo said. "She was up all night, praying."

Luis nodded. "The funeral is tomorrow."

The funeral. Ginny hadn't thought of that. Of course they would bury those pathetic bits of flesh and bone. She glanced again at Felicia, and saw tears glistening on her cheeks. Did she understand what they were saying? Perhaps not—Ginny knew something about that particular grief, how it chose its own moments, regardless of what else was going on.

Eduardo shifted in his chair and met Frank's eyes. "What have you come back for?"

"To ask more questions about your brother."

"We've already told you everything we know."

Frank nodded. "You realize that things have changed now. When I was here before I believed your brother might have gone off on his own. Now, of course, that's no longer the case."

"We told you there was no reason for him to go anywhere."

"Yes, you did."

"You didn't believe us."

"I may not believe you this time, either."

Nino's brothers looked at each other. Finally Eduardo shrugged. "Ask, then."

"I'll need to go over the same questions," Frank said, "and maybe some new ones. Now, the last time

Nino was here, did he bring anything for the children?"

It went on for an hour. Ginny scribbled until her fingers were stiff and her notes looked like chicken tracks. Frank went over the details of Nino's schedule, both when he had worked at Holiday Acres and when he had worked for the Forest Service, without learning anything new. Nino had usually left work on Friday afternoons, except during the harvest, when he worked on Saturday, too. He drove straight to Harmony, and stayed there until five on Monday morning, when he drove back to Galina. He had rarely talked about either of his jobs or about Holiday Acres. None of his family had ever been to Galina.

At noon Felicia went into the kitchen to start the family's meal. A few minutes later Frank lifted the coffeepot and poured the last drops into his cup.

"Felicia," Eduardo called. "*Más café.*"

"Here, let me do it." Ginny quickly stood and picked up the coffee tray. Felicia appeared at the kitchen door as she carried it in.

"You're busy cooking," Ginny said. "I can make the coffee."

Whether or not Felicia understood, she kept out of the way while Ginny filled the kettle and set it on a burner. A pot of beans simmered on the stove, their smell blending with the pungent scent of onions and chilies from a bowl on the counter. Felicia went back to work, making tortillas. She pinched a lump from a mound of *mása* dough, flattened it between her palms, slapped it into a flat round, and dropped it onto the griddle. She turned it once, then flipped it into a warming dish with a half dozen others and pinched out another lump of dough.

"May I try?" Ginny asked.

Felicia looked up, nodded, and handed her the dough. Ginny did her best to pat it out. Finally she held up her sorry-looking effort for Felicia's inspection.

Felicia smiled. She took the tortilla, expertly re-shaped it, and dropped it onto the griddle.

They watched the tortilla bake. Ginny could feel Felicia's eyes on her, but when she tried to meet them Felicia looked away. She searched desperately for something to say. Finally she spoke.

"I met your husband a few times."

"At the Forest Service?" Felicia asked. Her words were heavily accented, but clear.

Ginny nodded. Felicia flipped the tortilla, caught sight of her wedding ring, and stood looking at it. Ginny laid her hand on Felicia's. "I'm sorry," she said. "Very sorry. My husband died, too, five years ago."

Felicia took a deep breath. Her arm trembled under Ginny's touch. "I have thought now, for many days, that he must be dead."

Ginny nodded.

"Even Father Michael tried to tell me he had run away. It is better to know the truth."

The kettle began to whistle. Ginny lifted it off the stove while Felicia got the coffee out. They worked together, putting clean cups on the tray, refilling the cream and sugar. Ginny picked the tray up, ready to go back to the dining room. Felicia gently touched her arm, then turned to pinch out more dough for another tortilla.

Frank looked up as Ginny came back into the dining room. She gave him a little nod. She had spoken to Felicia Alvarez alone, and she had learned something. Later she would find out if it was what he wanted to know.

"Eduardo's going to show us around," Frank said. "We'll start with the house."

They followed Eduardo down the short hallway, stopping first at the room the two brothers shared. The beds were neatly made, the top of the single dresser clear except for family pictures. Felicia's room was fussier, with ruffled curtains at the window and a flowered bedspread. In the children's room a dozen dolls, some dressed in bright Mexican costumes, were lined up on a shelf below the window.

They went through the kitchen and into the double garage that had been converted into one large room, with its own door to the patio. Felicia's mother was there, a small, gray-haired woman dressed in black, sitting on a couch with the two girls. They watched in solemn-eyed silence as Frank and Ginny looked around. Part of the room was evidently used as an office—there was a desk, telephone, an adding machine, a file cabinet. At the other end was the grandmother's bed, with a crucifix on the wall above it.

"I see you've got a Christmas tree operation here," Frank said.

Eduardo nodded.

"When did you start that?"

"Five years ago. It was Nino's idea."

Frank wanted the details of the Alvarez business arrangements. Eduardo answered his questions with reluctance, but he did answer. The brothers had started with strawberries, added vegetables, and then Nino had suggested Christmas trees as a long-term crop. They would not have tried it without his experience—Nino gave advice and worked with them on the days he was home.

"You and Luis felt OK about that, taking advice from your little brother?"

Eduardo looked puzzled. "Nino knew everything about it. He had learned from his boss, Mr. Meissner."

"So the three of you got along just fine? No quarrels, no disagreements?"

"We had disagreements, of course. Myself, I did not want the Christmas trees, but Nino and Luis talked me into it."

"How's the business doing?"

Eduardo spread his hands. "Last year, we broke even. This year we may make a profit."

"Who does your taxes?"

"Nino."

"Could I see your copies of last year's forms?"

Eduardo shrugged, then went to the file cabinet and handed a folder to Frank.

Frank leafed through the papers, noting that the Alvarez brothers had formed a partnership to run their business. That tied their interests together more tightly than incorporation would have. He pulled a sheet from the folder and showed it to Ginny. On his personal tax form, Nino had once again claimed only himself as an exemption.

Suddenly Ginny knew. She knew why Nino's wife and children did not appear on the tax forms, why he had never spoken of them, why Felicia was afraid. She glanced at Frank. Had he guessed, too, that they were illegals? She couldn't tell from his expression.

Frank handed the file back to Eduardo. "We'd like to look around outside, too."

Eduardo led them out to the patio. He stopped at the edge and glanced down at his feet, clad only in socks.

"That's OK," Frank said. "We'd just as soon go by ourselves. We'll let you know when we're done."

Eduardo glared at him, clearly not liking the idea. He turned abruptly and went back into the house.

They walked slowly down the lane beside the poplar trees, glanced into the shed, then went on past Luis's tractor. Unlike Holiday Acres, the land here was flat, miles of muddy floodplain spreading east to the mountains. Ginny stooped to look at one of the little trees, holding a tightly furled bud against her palm. It was a balsam, one of the new variety Wes Meissner had introduced at Holiday Acres. That was interesting in itself, because she was pretty sure Wes had raised that stock from seed. It was not likely anyone was selling it commercially. She snapped off the tip of a branch and rolled it between her fingers, breathing in the clean, piny scent.

"What did you think of Felicia?" Frank asked.

Ginny was staring at the bit of balsam, her memory jogged by the smell. Frank repeated his question.

Ginny straightened up. "She knows more English than you think she does."

Frank nodded. "Do you think she's a wetback?"

"I think she's an illegal immigrant," Ginny said stiffly.

Frank glanced at her, amused. "OK, I stand corrected. What about the kids?"

"They're so young; they were probably born here, don't you think?" So he had guessed. Well, at least she had figured it out on her own.

"But he didn't claim them on the tax form, either, because someone might start wondering where the mother was."

"But if Nino married her, wouldn't she be eligible for citizenship?"

"Unless Nino was illegal, too. What I think," Frank said, starting to walk again, "is that the three Alvarez brothers are all here on phony papers. They might not even be from Mexico—maybe Nicaragua, El Salvador, one of those places."

"Refugees," Ginny murmured.

"Anyway, they all got here, but somehow they couldn't get papers for Felicia. Probably not for her mother, either. They don't dare talk to Immigration and Naturalization, for fear their own status will be jeopardized."

"It would explain why Felicia's so afraid," Ginny said. "You know, Frank, I may be pretty naive, but I just don't think these people are dealing drugs."

"I don't either, not now that we've got a good reason for why they've been so secretive. I just wish we could verify it."

"Father Michael," Ginny exclaimed.

"Who?"

"Felicia mentioned someone called Father Michael. I'll bet he's at that Catholic church we drove past."

Frank glanced at his watch. "It's worth a try. Let's pack it up here."

They stopped at the house to let Eduardo know they were leaving. Ginny had hoped to have a few more words with Felicia, but Nino's wife and daughters were nowhere in sight. She and Frank climbed into the truck and sat for a moment while the engine warmed up.

Ginny glanced idly through the rain at the station wagon and the battered pickup in the driveway. "Frank," she asked, "where's Nino's car?"

NINE

"NOW THAT," said Frank, "is a very good question. Especially from a brand-new deputy."

He looked amused. "What's so funny?" Ginny asked.

"Just that no one else has thought to ask. Not Sheriff Holt, or Deputy Wilcox, or anyone at Galina or the SO."

"But where is his car?"

"No one knows."

She thought for a moment. "Have I got this right? If I hadn't found Nino's body, no one would know he was dead."

"Ten-four."

"You were investigating him as a missing person."

"He was gone, and so was his car. I figured he'd gone off somewhere."

"Whoever killed him did something with the car."

Frank nodded. "Very good. You may get the hang of this business yet."

"You must have looked for it."

"The state police have a tracer out. We can check with them later today." He put the truck into gear. "Meanwhile, let's go find that church."

St. Mary's was a small but handsome brick building, put up about the turn of the century by the town's well-to-do Catholic minority. A discordant modern wing, tacked on many years later, was saved from ugliness by use of the same rosy local brick. Off to one side was a parish house, almost lost behind a laurel hedge.

They tried the church's front door but found it bolted, as Ginny had expected. They walked around the church, ducking under dripping cedar branches, to a smaller entrance. Here they had better luck. Though no one answered their knock, the door swung open with a little groan, and they stepped into a dim hallway that smelled faintly of mothballs. As they stood there, peering at the sickly yellow walls, they heard the shuffle of footsteps. A moment later a priest appeared at the far end of the hall. He flicked on the overhead light and came toward them, his slippers flapping softly as he walked.

"Hello. Can I help you?" He struck Ginny as far too young; the dog collar and dark shirt under a corduroy jacket emphasized his thin, stooped shoulders. He carried himself with authority, though, and the eyes behind his wire-rimmed glasses took in everything.

"We're looking for Father Michael," Frank said.

"I see. Immigration? No, police. Well, I'm Father Michael."

Frank put away the identification card the priest had not needed to see. "Frank Carver, federal agent for the

U.S. Forest Service. I'm investigating the death of one of your parishioners, Nino Alvarez.''

"Come into my office, then. It's just as dark, but at least it's warm.''

"Get him talking," Frank murmured as they followed Father Michael down the hall. He ushered them into a small room with a single window through which nothing could be seen but the darkly looming laurel hedge. An electric heater glowed beside his desk.

"Sit down, sit down. Nino Alvarez wasn't an active member of this parish, you understand. I really saw him only on holidays.''

"What about the rest of his family?" Ginny asked. She was sure he knew Felicia better, and she preferred to leave the questions about Nino to Frank.

"Felicia comes every Sunday, and Mrs. Gómez, her mother, comes for Wednesday mass as well. It's often like that, you know. The men leave religion to the women.''

Frank sat back, out of the way, as Ginny encouraged the priest to talk. He guessed that Father Michael, in spite of his apparent youth, was probably in his thirties. His immediate pigeonholing of them did not surprise Frank. People who were accustomed to dealing with officials, especially with the police, get so they could smell you coming. The reference to immigration was enlightening, too. Frank glanced around the little room, looking for confirmation of his suspicions, and found it in a pile of pamphlets on a corner of the desk.

Father Michael was interested in the sanctuary movement. Frank did not follow politics, but he did watch the television news, and he knew that some priests and nuns had been tried recently in Texas for smuggling refugees. A couple of years ago, too, his brother's boy, who had joined the Quakers, had ruined a family Thanksgiving with his opinions of U.S. involvement in Central America. The pamphlets bore the same slogans Robbie had been mouthing then.

Ginny was doing a good job of keeping Father Michael talking. When he sidestepped her question about where Mrs. Gómez was from, she did not press him but backed off to safer ground, expressing her sympathy for Felicia and the children. That was all right. She had given Frank time to figure out his approach.

He waited for a pause in the conversation. "I need to know more about the Alvarez family, Father. I've questioned them twice now, and I can tell they're hiding something."

Father Michael's expression was noncommittal. "Many people, even innocent people, might appear to the police to be hiding something."

"I'm investigating a murder. What they're hiding may or may not be relevant to that murder. If it's not, I'll leave them alone. I don't care about immigration or refugees or any of that stuff, except as it affects my investigation."

"Then I can assure you, Agent Carver, that it is not relevant."

"I'm afraid I'm the one who has to decide that. But I mean what I said: if they're illegals, it's none of my business. They're not going to tell me. I'd rather find out from you than from I and N."

It was a deliberately unpleasant suggestion. Father Michael looked out the window, then back again. "Felicia and her mother have no papers."

"I take it that Nino wasn't square with the law, either?"

"What does it matter, now that he's dead?"

Frank had never felt that answering a question meant he had lost control of an interview. The men who had trained him—tough Los Angeles cops, most of them—had thought differently. Never let a suspect get on top, they said, and to them everyone was a suspect. Frank had found he could often learn more by winning a witness's cooperation. He set out now to do that with Father Michael.

"All right, what does it matter? Let's assume Alvarez was in this country illegally. Let's assume he was a refugee. Is it possible that someone could have come here to kill him for political reasons? That's the kind of thing I need to know."

Father Michael nodded thoughtfully. "Do you have any reason to think his death was political?"

"Not yet. But if nobody's talking about his past, then I do."

"I see. And then Immigration and Naturalization would get involved."

"Most likely. A whole heap of other people, too."

Father Michael sighed. "Well, I also have no reason to believe Nino was killed for political reasons. He had been in this country a long time, ten years I think. His father was killed by soldiers in their country—they claimed he was a Communist."

"Which country was that?"

Father Michael did not want to tell him. "Guatemala," he finally said. "The people who killed Nino's father are probably dead themselves, by now."

Frank went on with the questioning. Clearly, a number of refugees had been in the area for some time. They were there because it was safe. If Nino's death had anything to do with Central American politics, Father Michael would have known and, Frank believed, would have told them.

"The Alvarez brothers are doing pretty well at their business?" Frank asked, changing the subject.

"From what I hear, yes. They've worked hard."

"They get along? No quarrels?"

"Eduardo and Luis are not saints, Mr. Carver, and neither was Nino. But they got along."

"Felicia Alvarez is an attractive woman," Frank said. "The three brothers all lived in the same house with her. You weren't aware of any tension, any rivalry?"

"Not what you mean, no. I might add that Eduardo has a long-standing arrangement with an older woman in town, and that for the past year Luis has been courting one of my parishioners."

Frank asked a few more questions, but Father Michael could add little to what they already knew. One lead pursued to a dead end, one possibility scratched out. He thanked Father Michael and let the priest see them to the door. Outside, the morning's steady drizzle had lifted. Frank glanced at his watch. If they picked up hamburgers and ate them in the truck, they could just make it to Holiday Acres for their appointment with Susie Meissner.

"THERE'S ONE THING I don't understand," Ginny said, wiping catsup from her fingers half an hour later. "Why did you stop investigating Nino's disappearance after you talked to his family the first time?"

"Because I thought they knew where he was. Look, a week after Nino disappeared you got that phone call from some guy who said he was Nino's cousin. Probably Eduardo. He was worried, right?"

Ginny nodded.

"But when I got there a couple of days later, no one in the family would talk to me. So I figured that by then they knew Nino was OK, but was doing something risky, maybe illegal, and they realized the phone call had been a mistake. Well, hell, I didn't care what Alvarez was up to, so long as it didn't involve the Forest Service, so I dropped it."

"And what do you think now?"

"I think they were terrified that someone might be after the whole family."

"But you told Father Michael you didn't think it was political!"

"I don't. Eduardo and Luis have had a month to run and hide, but what are they doing? Harvesting Christmas trees as though nothing was wrong. They aren't afraid anymore."

Ginny nodded. "So we're back where we were yesterday."

"Except that we've learned a few things. Did you notice the equipment in that shed?"

"It looked like the usual stuff."

"Right. The usual stuff they use at Holiday Acres."

Ginny whistled. "I wonder! He could have been walking off with things for years. Maybe Len is right about him." She paused. "I did notice the balsams."

"The balsams?"

"A lot of the Alvarez trees are balsams. Wes Meissner planted a few thousand of them before he died."

"Really? Tell me more."

"Well, Wes wanted to try something new, get an edge on the market. Balsams are raised for Christmas trees in Europe, but no one had ever tried it around here. He got some seeds and started them himself. Most growers buy seedlings, so setting up his own nursery was a pretty big investment."

"What's so special about balsams?"

"They're different. The color, the shape, the smell. People want something a little different. You can ask Harriet. She'll tell you all about it."

"And some of the Alvarez trees are balsams?"

"Almost half. As far as I know, there's only one place they could have come from."

FRANK PULLED OVER when they reached the top of the pass leading into the Neskanie Valley. Radio reception could be spotty on the other side, and he wanted to check on the tracer he had put on Alvarez's car. He called the county dispatcher in Longmont and waited. Gusty winds shook the truck, spitting rain against the windows. They could see the road and the nearby hills, but the valley below was shrouded in clouds.

The dispatcher had nothing to report. Frank asked to have the search extended to Washington and California, then put the truck into gear and moved back out onto the road.

He glanced at Ginny. "Where would you dump a car, if you wanted to make sure no one ever found it?"

"Drive it over a cliff into the ocean," she replied.

"Any place around here you could do that?"

"Lots. I can think of half a dozen, right offhand."

He nodded, remembering his drive down the coast in August. The road ran along miles of sheer, rocky headlands that plunged straight into the water. Behind them the dense forest ran inland for miles. The few towns, little more than fishing villages, did a brisk tourist trade during the summer, but in late October the highway would be deserted. He had stopped to stretch his legs at a dozen viewpoints. A car could have disappeared over any of them with almost no trace.

"Write down the places you can think of. We'll get a list to the state police."

"Needle in a haystack," Ginny said.

Frank agreed with a gloomy nod.

HARRIET WHITTAKER met them at the door, dressed today in jeans and a worn flannel shirt, her hair tucked up under a scarf. She led them through the house to the kitchen. Susie was sitting at the big table, wrapped in a voluminous robe, drinking hot chocolate. She looked pale and tired.

Frank had expected Harriet to insist on being present while they questioned her daughter. She surprised him, though. "I'll be out with the crew," she said, squeezing Susie's shoulder. "Magda can get me on the radio if you need anything." She pulled on a pair of muddy boots and left by the back door.

Frank watched her go. He had questions for her, too. In fact, since talking to Casey Mullen at his trailer he had questions for everyone who lived at Holiday Acres. But he would start with Susie.

She was big-boned, like her mother, but where Harriet was spare, Susie's frame was softly padded. Her lanky hair was pulled back with pink barrettes, and the skin around her eyes was puffy from tears.

"You understand, Miss Meissner, that we're investigating Nino Alvarez's death? Did you know him well?"

"Of course I knew him. He worked here for years."

"Would you have called him a friend?"

"He was more Danny's friend, I guess."

Frank pressed on, working hard for every bit of information. Like the others, Susie had not known about Nino's family; she had visited his cabin at Holiday Acres once or twice, but had never seen any pictures or letters, nothing personal, just his clothes and a few books. He had a crucifix on the wall, she remembered that. As far as she knew everyone had liked him, except maybe Len. Yes, she thought her mother had depended on Nino a lot, but she really didn't know, she just took care of the house.

"When was the last time you saw him?"

Susie had been on the edge of crying for at least five minutes. Now she began to sob. Frank waited. Manic-depressive, her mother had said. Was this the sort of thing she meant?

Susie yanked some tissues from a box on the table and made an effort to pull herself together. "It's all so awful," she said. "It's just so awful."

Frank restated his question. "Can you recall the last time you saw him?"

She shook her head. "Not really. I helped him load some stuff into his car when he moved out of the cabin, and after that I guess I saw him once or twice in town."

"Did he ever come back to Holiday Acres after that?"

She stared at the floor. "Not as far as I know."

He was not satisfied, but pushing her would lead to more tears, and probably end any effective questioning. The suspicion that she was lying, though, made him a little less gentle. "What were you doing up on Jackson Ridge on Halloween night?"

Susie's head jerked up. "How do you know that?"

"What were you doing up there?"

"I went up to the old lookout. I like to go there sometimes."

"And your mother followed you?"

Ginny's automatic pencil stabbed into the paper, breaking the lead. It wasn't fair to pick on Susie, everyone picked on her. She twirled more lead down and set her jaw. Frank had to push, but she did not have to like it.

"I was upset about something." Susie pursed her lips. "Mother knew it, and then I guess when she couldn't find me she figured I'd gone up there."

"What did you do at the lookout?"

"We just talked, that's all."

Her voice had an angry, stubborn edge. Frank backed off, trying a different approach. "There were some other people on Jackson Ridge that night. We're trying to figure out who was up there then. Can you remember when you reached the lookout?"

Susie thought for a moment. "Not exactly, maybe about eight thirty or nine. I wasn't paying much attention."

"And your mother joined you later? How much later? Fifteen minutes?"

"About that. We talked for maybe half an hour, then we went home."

"Did you see anyone else while you were up there?"

"I think we passed another car on the road, but I'm not sure."

She was calmer now. Frank waited a moment, then started on the third and final area he had planned to explore. "I understand you've been under medical care, Miss Meissner. I hope it's nothing serious?"

Susie ducked her head and stared at the floor. When she finally looked up she gave them a miserable, embarrassed little smile.

What on earth was going on? Ginny had never seen Susie act this way before. Awkward, yes, uncomfortable, socially inept—but never ashamed, never secretive. What could Susie—at the doctor's—Ginny looked up, her eyes widening in realization.

Susie smiled at her, the first direct, genuine smile of pleasure Ginny had ever seen on her face. She looked different, too, now that Ginny was paying attention. Her skin was soft, almost glowing, her eyes were bright in spite of the puffiness, and the hands clasped around her belly were at rest, no longer fidgety.

"OK," Frank said, "I'm starting to get the picture. Would one of you care to clue me in?"

Ginny caught the pleading look in Susie's eyes. "You're going to have a baby, aren't you?"

Susie nodded. "I'm not supposed to tell anyone."

"You're not going to be able to keep it a secret much longer," Ginny said. "I'd guess you're about three months along?"

Susie nodded again.

"And the visit to the doctor yesterday?" Frank asked.

"Mother wanted me to have an abortion."

But Susie had not gone through with it. Ginny could guess what it must have taken to defy her mother. She leaned over and touched Susie's arm. "What happened?"

Susie tightened her hands around her belly. "Mother made the appointment and drove me in. She said it was just for an exam. The doctor talked to us, but whenever he asked me something, she answered. Finally I figured out what was going on. They took me into a little room and had me lay down. Mother wanted to stay but they made her leave, and then the nurse started getting all this equipment out, and telling me everything would be OK."

Susie's voice rose as she spoke, her words coming out faster and faster. She glanced nervously at the back door. Ginny touched her arm again. "What happened then?"

"I sat up and said, 'No, no, I want the baby.' Then the nurse called the doctor in and they both talked to me, and then the doctor told Mother he couldn't do the abortion. He talked to her a long time—I stayed in the little room with the nurse. She told me about being pregnant, and having the baby, and everything. I really liked her."

"Is this what you and your mother talked about that night at the lookout?" Frank asked.

"No." Susie shook her head. "I knew then, but I didn't tell her."

"When did you tell her?"

"A couple of days ago."

"How does Harriet feel about it now?" Ginny asked.

"I think it's OK." Susie frowned. "She's being nice to me, anyway."

Ginny squeezed her hand. "And you're glad, I can tell. I'm really happy for you, Susie. Rebecca will be thrilled."

Susie grinned. "It's going to be a big surprise to a lot of people, I guess."

"Susie," Frank asked, "why didn't you tell Harriet sooner?"

She faltered, then looked at the floor again. "I guess I kept thinking he'd come back."

"Who would come back?"

"Nino." She fell silent, biting her lip. "Mother's going to kill me for telling," she added with satisfaction.

TEN

THEY SPENT ANOTHER HOUR at Holiday Acres, getting the full story from Susie. Frank should have been happy with the new light she shed on Alvarez, but it had been a long day. He was hungry, and the hungrier he got the grouchier he felt. He grumbled as he asked the same questions over again, even though the answers were more interesting this time around.

Susie spoke slowly at first, in a halting voice. She had been attracted to Nino, it appeared, because he was nice to her. Ginny's hand faltered as Susie described the common courtesy she had taken for special attention. She had pursued him for over a year, keeping every hint of her interest secret from Harriet. She thought Danny had known something was going on; Danny and Nino were friends and spent a lot of time together.

Then Len had moved in and started picking on Nino. Finding fault with his work, saying he was too familiar with the family. Susie thought he was jealous of Nino, because Harriet trusted him so much.

Did she think Nino had embezzled ten thousand dollars?

"No!" she said in astonishment. "Who said that? Is that how Len got Mother to fire him?"

Frank raised his eyebrows. "You didn't know?"

"They don't tell me anything about the business. I knew Len wanted Nino gone, but no one ever said anything about ten thousand dollars."

"And you? Did you want Nino gone?"

Susie looked miserable again. "I could tell he was relieved to get away from me."

Frank had been doing some calculations. "You must have gotten pregnant after Nino left Holiday Acres."

"We kept seeing each other, mostly when I insisted. He was doing it to be nice, but I guess I thought that was better than nothing."

"SHE FELL IN LOVE because he was nice to her," Ginny said as they drove back to the station. "That's one of the saddest things I've ever heard."

"I don't know," Frank said. He was still grouchy, and ready to argue. "There are plenty of worse reasons to fall in love."

"Such as?" Ginny asked.

"Because a man's tough, and beats you up. Because he's weak, and you can dominate him. Because he's sick, and you can take care of him."

"Any more?"

"There must be hundreds."

Ginny silently added one more. Because he's there, and there isn't anyone else. She stared glumly out the window during the rest of the drive back to the station.

There was a message on her desk from the SO. The forest supervisor wanted to make sure Frank would be

available for a conference on Monday morning—
Hunsaker himself, Sheriff Holt, and some law enforcement hotshots from the regional office would be
there.

Ginny and Frank spent Saturday at the deserted
ranger station, preparing a report for the conference.
It was an excellent summary, but Ginny had to agree
when Frank slapped his notes down in disgust, ex-
claiming that all they had done so far was get some of
the underbrush out of the way.

"We need a break," Frank said. "My head feels like
it's been stuffed."

"Dinner at the café?"

"Is there anywhere else?"

It was a serious question. The food at the Galina
Café was good, but Frank had been eating little else for
days. "Let me call home," Ginny suggested.

Alice was just starting dinner. "Bring him on over,"
she said. "We should be ready to eat in an hour."

The telephone rang as they were going out the door.
Ginny answered, then held the receiver out to Frank.
"Harriet Whittaker."

Frank lifted an eyebrow, but Ginny shook her head.
She did not know what Harriet wanted. He took the
phone. "Hello, Mrs. Whittaker. What can I do for
you?"

Harriet's voice was audible in the room, small and
tinny. Frank listened intently for a few minutes. "Can
you tell me more about the car?" He made some notes

on a piece of paper. "All right, Mrs. Whittaker. I'll see what I can do. Thanks for calling."

He set the phone down and looked up with satisfaction. "Two men Harriet doesn't know came to the house an hour ago, looking for Danny. He wasn't there, so they waited in their car. An expensive rental, by the way. When Danny arrived they got out and talked to him for a few minutes. Then Danny got into their car and they all drove off again."

"Harriet sounded upset."

"She didn't like the men—they wouldn't tell her what they wanted, they refused to come in, they refused to leave. They pretty much called the shots. Danny didn't look happy to see them, either. Oh, and she thinks they may have been there before, about a month ago. She's worried."

"What does she want you to do?"

"Look for them, presumably." He picked up the phone again. "First I'll call the sheriff's office with a description of the car. You stay here, on the radio, in case I need help."

"You shouldn't go alone."

"Not much choice, is there?"

Ginny bristled, but then her fire training took over. This was a time to follow orders, not question them. And Frank was right; she would be more useful on the radio.

Frank got through to the sheriff's office and gave them a description of the car. "Better pass it on to the state police. Find out which company it's from, too."

As soon as he set the phone down it rang again. "Carver here. Hello, Mrs. Whittaker. OK, can I talk to Danny?"

There was a pause, then Frank talked to Harriet again. He covered the receiver with his hand and looked up at Ginny. "He's back. Holiday Acres is on the way to your place, isn't it?"

Ginny nodded.

"Mrs. Whittaker. We'll be there in about twenty minutes. Don't let him leave."

He hung up. "You copy, Deputy?"

Ginny nodded. "Wouldn't Danny talk to you?"

"No way. We'll just have to see the man ourselves."

SHE DROVE her own car, following Frank down the Neskanie highway and Tenmile Road. He pulled over at the foot of the Holiday Acres driveway and motioned for her to get in.

"The sheriff's office just radioed. The car came from a company with ties to organized crime. Looks like Danny's running with a pretty rough crowd."

Ginny felt sick. "But what would Danny..."

Frank put the truck into gear and started up the driveway. "That," he said grimly, "is what we are going to ask him."

"LISTEN, DANNY," Frank said, leaning forward. "I don't know who those men are, but I can sure as hell find out. Why not just tell me, right now."

"Because it's none of your damn business," Danny snapped. They were in the Holiday Acres office—Danny, Frank, and Ginny—with the door closed. Harriet, looking very worn, had let them in, then gone to the living room to wait with Len.

"Are they friends of yours?"

Danny glared at him.

"If they are, I don't think much of your choice of friends. If they're not, I might be able to help you."

"I don't need your help."

"When you're playing with those guys, Danny, you need all the help you can get."

"Listen, Carver." Danny's voice was colder than Ginny had ever heard it. "I don't have to answer your questions. Your job is to find out who killed Nino Alvarez. Well, it wasn't me. So keep out of my business."

Frank glared back. "Your business is quickly becoming my business."

Danny folded his arms across his chest. "I don't have anything else to say."

Frank waited for a minute, then another. The room was silent. Danny turned his head to look out the window.

Frank sighed. "Have it your way, then." He got up, looked at Danny one more time, then left the room.

Ginny stayed in her chair. After a minute Danny turned to face her.

"I thought you were my friend."

She bit her lip. "I thought so, too."

"Some friend."

"Danny, who were those men? What's going on? Can't you see Harriet's worried sick?"

"Screw Harriet."

She closed her eyes. "I'm sorry," she murmured. When she opened them again Danny was still watching her. "Is there anything I can do?"

"It's a little late to ask, don't you think?"

"I'm asking, Danny. Is there anything I can do to help you?"

"I just wish you weren't involved in this. They had no right, making you do it."

"I accepted the job. I'm going to do the best I can."

"Yeah," he said morosely. "You always do."

She left Danny staring out the window and went to find Frank. He was in the living room, talking with Harriet and Len.

"If they come back, call me. Immediately. Call me if Danny says anything about them."

"Don't worry, we'll call." Len tightened his arm around Harriet's shoulders. "Damn kid. He's got no business treating his mother like this."

Harriet was sobbing quietly. Frank touched Ginny's arm and they left. At the foot of the driveway they stopped to pick up Ginny's car.

"Did he say anything after I left?" Frank asked.

"I asked if there was anything I could do to help. He said no." She paused. "Do you know what's going on?"

"If Danny's friends are who I think they are, it's probably drugs. Did you say he worked in a lab?"

"When he's working. It's been on and off."

"You said he was busted for pot."

She nodded. "Back in high school. A few years ago he told me he wasn't doing it anymore. But I really couldn't say, Frank. Since he got out of college we haven't seen him that much."

Frank grunted.

"Is he in trouble?" she asked.

"He's in trouble with me, I'll tell you that." Frank sighed and leaned back in his seat. "Looks like another late night."

"You want me to go back to the station with you?"

"No, mostly I'll be on the phone. Thanks, though."

"Well, Alice's dinner is still waiting."

ALICE CAME TO THE DOOR as they pulled up. She was a tall woman with a plain, angular face, and Frank felt her eyes on him as soon as he got out of the car. He waited for Ginny to make the introductions.

Alice wiped her hands on her apron. "I'm glad to meet you, Mr. Carver. I hear you can be grouchy at times."

Frank swallowed, feeling suddenly about ten years old. "I'm afraid that's true."

"Well, you've got no business being grouchy with Ginny. She's got enough problems."

"Alice," Ginny warned as they went inside. "Where's Rebecca?"

"Upstairs doing homework. Here she comes."

There was a loud clatter on the stairs, and Rebecca piled into the dining room. "Is he here? Is he here?" She caught sight of Frank and fell silent.

Ginny introduced them. Rebecca was as thin and squirmy as Frank remembered his own daughters at that age. Her hair was neatly combed, and she was wearing a t-shirt smudged with paint. "Are you a painter?" he asked.

She looked down at her shirt. "We've been doing a project at school." She looked up at Ginny, suddenly very earnest. "Mom, you've got to help me. I told everyone I'm drawing a picture of Bigfoot, but it won't come out right."

Ginny smiled. "What? Even though you've seen one?"

"You've seen a Bigfoot?" Frank asked.

Rebecca nodded. "Right out there by the creek, Mr. Carver. That's what I'm doing my project on." She turned to Ginny again. "I asked Aunt Alice, and Susie, too, but they both say they can't draw. You'll help me, won't you?"

"Sure. We'll use your magic eye. But not tonight. It's late, and we're all hungry."

"That's the truth," Alice said. "Young lady, you may come into the kitchen and help with the salad." They left the room, and Frank was alone with Ginny.

"Nice kid," he said. "What's the magic eye?"

"Oh, it's just a game we play."

He was surprised to see her look a little embarrassed. "What kind of game?"

"Well, it's silly, really. We pretend I'm drawing something Rebecca sees with her magic eye, inside her mind. Of course, I just draw what she describes. Sometimes, though, it is a little eerie."

Frank was quiet for a moment. "I think it could be possible."

"You do?"

He nodded slowly. "There can be a connection, when two people are close. I've felt something like that with one of my daughters."

Fishing with Laurie. It had not happened often, but there had been times when he knew she had a strike, even though she was out of sight, a hundred yards downstream. Once he had even felt her play the fish in, reach out with the net, then lose it at the last moment. Nothing like that had ever happened with Rose, his other daughter. But then, Rose had never loved to fish.

He looked wistful. "How old were they—" Ginny started, and then didn't quite know how to finish the question. Which one of them had left? Somehow, she couldn't see Frank walking out on his family.

"When Minnie finally packed up? They were in high school. I was there for the best years." He paused, then smiled sheepishly. "Of course, now I wish I'd spent more time with them. Most fathers do, I guess, when their kids are grown."

"You have grandkids, though, don't you?" She wanted to comfort him, somehow, let him know she understood the choices he'd had to make. Only when she caught his quick, stung look did she realize she had, in effect, called him an old man.

"Three," he said gruffly.

Damn! She would have given anything, just then, to take the question back. She didn't care about his age. She liked him. She liked the wrinkles around his eyes and the bit of gravel in his voice. An awkward silence settled between them. "Like a glass of wine?" she asked.

"Sure, that would be great."

He prowled around the room while she filled two glasses. She handed him one.

"Thanks. How long have you lived here?"

"Almost twelve years."

"Nice place." He stopped in front of a framed drawing. Suddenly he chuckled. He was looking at a crew of mice, dressed as loggers in hard hats, suspenders, and caulk boots. They were hard at work in a forest of grass stems. He peered at the signature, then glanced at Ginny. "Nice."

"Dale had it framed. It was one of his favorites."

She stepped up to look at the drawing with him, letting her shoulder brush against the rough cloth of his jacket sleeve. Her head came just past his collar. He could smell her hair, faintly scented with soap.

"Dale was your husband?"

She nodded. "He died in a car accident a few years ago."

There was another silence. "I'm sorry," Frank said.

Ginny shrugged. "Thanks."

Alice came in then, carrying a casserole dish. Rebecca brought the salad, and dinner was ready. Frank followed Ginny to the table. Could she be twenty years younger? At least that, he thought gloomily, watching her sit down. Young enough to make him feel like a very old man.

He stayed for an hour after dinner, playing cards. This was Rebecca's suggestion. It turned out that she was a dynamite hearts player, ready to shoot the moon on even the slimmest chance of success. Frank, however, had not played poker twice a month for the past fifteen years without learning a few tricks of his own. Soon the game sharpened to a contest between the two of them, with Ginny and Alice staying in just to keep things rolling.

"Gotcha," Frank finally said, laying down his last cards.

"One more game," Rebecca demanded.

"Oh, no. I'm going to quit while I'm ahead."

"Just one more, Mr. Carver. Please?"

Frank laughed. "You are certainly a persistent young lady."

"Come on, Rebecca," Ginny said, smiling. "Mr. Carver has a long drive home."

"You'll come back, though, won't you? Mom never wants to play."

"I don't blame her, with a cardsharp like you."

"Oh, no. I never cheat."

"She just goes for the throat," said Ginny, standing up. "Let me get your coat, Frank, and I'll walk you to the car."

The night air felt cool on Ginny's face after the overheated dining room. The rain had stopped, and the clouds were breaking up. A light breeze rustled through the bare bushes near the creek. Frank was silent, a little withdrawn now, after the easy familiarity of the card game. Ginny could think of no way to apologize for her earlier blunder that would not simply make it worse. She only hoped that the good time they had had would make up for any hurt feelings.

Frank stopped beside the car door. "Thanks, Ginny." He wanted to take her hand, but didn't quite dare. Not an old grandfather like himself. "Alice is a great cook, and that kid of yours is too smart by half."

"I'm glad you came." She paused, cleared her throat, found she didn't have anything to add.

Frank could barely see her shadowed face, but he was acutely aware that only a few inches separated them. He opened the door and got in. "See you Monday."

She nodded. She needed a break, but suddenly she wished tomorrow was a regular work day, and that she would be seeing him in the morning. Frank got his rig started and drove off, his taillights disappearing around the bend. Still Ginny stood there, listening to Tenmile River gurgle past on its way to join the Neskanie.

ON SUNDAY Alice drove Ginny and Rebecca out to her house on the coast. She needed to check her house-plants and pick up the mail, and besides, she said, it would do Ginny good to get out of telephone reach for a day.

"I like your Mr. Carver," Alice said as they left the Neskanie River and headed south along the coast. "He's working you too hard, though."

"You liked him? I'd never have guessed."

"Sure. And he likes you, which I don't think you've noticed."

"Alice, I'm just working for him."

"So? That means he can't like you?"

Ginny had to admit that the outing did her good. She woke up Monday morning feeling rested for the first time in almost a week. She gave herself the luxury of being a few minutes late for work, knowing that Frank would not be there. When she hung her jacket up, she noticed Len's coat on the rack. He had been spending mornings at Holiday Acres lately, so that was a bit of a surprise. He had started the coffee, too, which was even more unusual.

She was just sitting down at the typewriter when he came in. "Carver's out this morning?"

"He's got a meeting at the SO."

"How about doing your performance appraisal to-day? Get it out of the way."

She picked up her coffee cup and followed him across the hall to his office. Everyone in the Forest Service had a performance appraisal twice a year. Len usually scheduled one for early December, after fire season was wrapped up. Her job description was broken up into elements, which were weighted for importance. This morning, just as he had done before, Len graded her on each one, asking her opinion as they went along. To her surprise, he added a recommendation for a bonus for her handling of the Cripple Elk burn while he was gone. Ginny was pleased—she had never gotten a bonus before.

Len stacked the papers and put them to one side. "How's it going on the new detail? Things working out OK?"

"It's a lot of overtime. More than I'm used to."

"That's law enforcement. How's Carver treating you?"

"It was a little rough at first, but we're getting along OK."

"You doing the clerical end?"

"Most of it. Some investigative work, too." That would look good on her appraisal, and she wanted Len to know it.

"Oh? What's he got you doing?"

"Handling evidence, what we've got, anyhow. Asking questions when we talk to people. Mostly, though, he's got me thinking, using what I know about Galina."

Len nodded. "I'm glad to hear it. That's one of the purposes of a detail, to get you a little cross-training. How's the case coming along?"

She hesitated. "I don't think I'm supposed to talk about it."

"Of course not. Any investigation has to remain confidential until it's finished. I just wondered how you were feeling about the job."

"To tell the truth, it's pretty frustrating right now."

"It must be tough. No motive, no likely suspect. No witnesses, either, from what I hear."

"Nino left the tavern about six on Halloween night. After that, he seems to have just disappeared until I found his body."

"He had that appointment with Harriet."

"But he didn't show up."

"Does Carver know anything about those gangster friends of Danny's?" Len asked. "Maybe there's a connection."

She hesitated again. "I'm really not supposed to talk about it."

"I understand. It's Harriet I'm worried about. Pretty hard on her if her son's accused of murder."

She looked up. "You think Danny killed Nino?"

"Now, don't get me wrong. I'm not making any accusations. He does seem the most likely suspect, but you'd know more about that than I do. I'm just thinking about Harriet."

"How is she?" Ginny asked. "She looked pretty low the other night."

"She's doing OK, so far." Len shook his head. "She is one tough lady, let me tell you. But the strain is getting to her."

Ginny stood up. "It's getting to all of us, I'm afraid."

Len nodded sympathetically. "I've heard maybe half the murders in this country are never solved."

"Those aren't very good odds, are they?"

She left Len's office and went back to her desk, where she started in on a pile of routine paperwork. As she typed she kept seeing the lines of trees at the Alvarez place. She had snapped off a twig and rolled it between her hands, releasing the fresh piny scent. Her fingers went to her nose, but this morning all she smelled was coffee and a faint trace of soap. The balsams did not smell quite the same as the firs—if you sniffed one, then the other, you could tell them apart. The needles and buds were shaped differently too. She typed some more, but something kept nagging at the back of her mind. Finally she rolled the last sheet out of the typewriter, separated out the various colored copies, and went into the little office she had turned over to Frank.

She unlocked the desk drawer, pulled out the daily diary file, and added the set she had just finished. In the back of the drawer was the folder from the Salem crime lab that had come in on Friday. In it were prints of the pictures Frank had taken at the scene of the crime.

She slipped the folder out and went through the photos without finding what she was looking for—the green tip of a branch, clinging to a muddy bit of plastic. Had she seen it that day, or was she thinking of all the Christmas trees she *had* seen lately, or perhaps the trimmings in the Holiday Acres packing shed and on the floor of Nino's old cabin? Here was the photograph of Nino's shoe, the last item they had found before calling off the search. Mud, black plastic, but no green twig with the bud tightly furled.

She put the photos back. As she was locking the desk she smelled scent and looked up. Maureen was standing in the doorway, the dispatch log in her hand.

ELEVEN

MAUREEN SET THE LOGBOOK on Ginny's desk. "I thought you might want to go over this," she said, flopping down into the empty chair. "I never have time to do all the entries."

Ginny opened the log. Maureen did not care enough to make time, that was the problem. She glanced down at the other woman's handwriting, big and sloppy, taking up twice as much room as it needed.

"So how do you like law enforcement?" Maureen asked.

"It's a change. How's dispatch going?"

"All right. Like you say, it's a change."

"Getting along with Len? He can be a real pain."

"Oh, he's not so bad."

"Has he been pulling the hand-on-the-shoulder routine?" Ginny asked. "I just hate it when he does that."

Maureen laughed. "He's behaving himself." She paused. "Your new boss looks pretty good."

"Frank? He's OK to work for."

"That's not quite what I meant. He seems to have taken a shine to you."

"Come on, Maureen."

"Seriously, Ginny. I've seen him watch you, and, I mean, he pays attention."

"Maureen, Frank Carver must be over fifty."

"So?" Maureen chuckled. "Do you know why he left Seattle?"

"He took early retirement."

"You mean you haven't heard about his last case?"

"He's mentioned it," Ginny said cautiously.

"Everybody's talking about it. Your new boss and his partner were investigating some kind of drug gang, and the gang killed the partner's daughter, as a warning, I guess."

Frank had not told her that. She waited, imagining how the gossip would trickle from Seattle—through clerks, secretaries, administrators—until it found Frank here in Galina. Now she would play her part by listening.

Maureen went on. "Carver was in charge of the investigation. They got the killers, too. Then when they went to court it looked like they were going to get off. Some kind of goof on Carver's part—no search warrant for the gun, something like that. So Carver's partner walked into the courtroom one morning and shot the two guys."

"No! He killed them?"

"Dead as doornails," said Maureen with satisfaction. "Now Carver's partner is locked up in a mental ward. I guess they let Carver retire instead of firing him."

Had Frank felt some responsibility for the girl's death? Ginny thought she knew him well enough to answer that question. Then, on top of that, he had left Seattle in disgrace. No wonder he had been willing to come to a backwater place like the Neskanie. Ginny hardly listened as Maureen rattled on about Frank's divorce, and how someone in the regional office had questioned his competency.

"Now Larry's wondering if he's still got what it takes," Maureen said. "Carver just doesn't seem to know what he's doing."

"He does too know what he's doing." Ginny glared at her. "Besides, how do you know what Larry Hunsaker thinks?"

"His secretary told me," Maureen said smugly.

Ginny had never liked Maureen, but this was the first time she had wanted to bash her face in. She wished desperately for something mean and hurtful to throw back, but there was nothing. Though Maureen was always ready to gossip, she kept her mouth shut about her own affairs.

"Maureen?" Len stuck his head in the doorway. "Ah, you are in there. Do you have time to go over those budget items now?"

Maureen got up and followed Len out of Dispatch, her hips swaying gently as she crossed the hall. There was a murmur of voices, and then, just as the door shut behind them, Len's hand slipped down onto Maureen's shoulder.

Ginny glared at the closed door. "That woman deserves Len Whittaker for a boss," she muttered.

FRANK STOMPED INTO Dispatch a little after noon, dropped his briefcase on the floor, and sank gloomily into a chair. Ginny watched with dismay. The session at the SO must have been worse than he had expected.

"We've got a week," he growled.

"Oh?"

"A week to make definite progress, or the regional office is taking over."

"What happens if they take over?"

"Zip is what happens. I'm back on timber theft, you're back talking to idiots on the radio, and the case is effectively closed."

"Oh, no. Frank, what did they say at the meeting? What do you mean, the case would be closed?"

"Hunsaker's mostly concerned about adverse publicity, and so far they're handling that OK. Sheriff Holt is happy so long as he doesn't have to do anything. And Phillips, the regional honcho, wants to shut us down before we go over budget. At the moment, I'd say you and I are the only people who care what happens."

"Us and the murderer."

"That's right. Gets kind of personal, doesn't it?" Frank glanced up at her. "Anything happen while I was gone?"

"I got the diaries typed, and Len did my performance appraisal." She frowned. Len always wanted to know every detail of what happened on the district.

"Something wrong?" Frank asked. "Len didn't give you a low rating, did he?"

"No. In fact, he recommended me for a bonus."

"Good." Frank heaved himself out of the chair. "Hate to lose my deputy just before the case falls to pieces. Let's get some lunch, then we'll go over our notes again. Somewhere in all that paper there's got to be something we can use."

LUNCH WAS a dismal affair. The stew at the Galina Café was overcooked, and the drizzle outside seemed to have become a permanent fixture. Frank's frown was even deeper when they got back to work. They started with his initial investigation of Nino's disappearance, wringing everything they could from it.

"Let's take it in order," Frank said. "Four weeks after Alvarez disappeared you found his body. Tell me exactly what you saw and did."

Ginny went through the story again, for the ninth or tenth time. When she got to the part where she recognized the hat, Frank stopped her.

"How did you know it was a Holiday Acres hat? You must have been, what, a hundred feet away at least."

"I just knew, Frank. I saw the piece of red cloth there where it didn't belong, and suddenly I remembered the last time I'd seen Nino, and how he always wore that hat, even when he was supposed to have a hard hat on. And I knew."

Frank shook his head. "It keeps pointing to that damn tree farm. The hat, the appointment with Harriet, Danny bringing his name up at that dinner party."

"And Susie's pregnancy."

"Most of all Susie's pregnancy. But none of it's concrete. I just wish someone had seen him there the night he disappeared."

He sighed and pulled out the next file, the photos of the search area. "It feels pointless to go over this stuff again and again, but it's all we've got."

"Frank." Ginny hesitated, then went on. "I looked through those photos this morning. I thought I'd remembered something. When we found the shoe, just before dark that day, do you remember some twigs stuck to it? I looked at the photos, but I didn't see anything."

Frank propped his cheek on his fist and thought. His natural memory had always been good, and he had been training it for twenty years.

"Yeah, I do remember something. Well, it ought to be here." He thumbed through the prints, came to one of the shoe and looked up, puzzled. "I thought I took two of this."

A tingle of excitement ran down Ginny's neck. "Did you?"

"Yeah, I think so." He flipped a few of the photos over to show the numbers inked on the back. "There should be forty-two prints. Number forty-one is missing."

She held her breath. "Did someone take it?"

"Now that would be dramatic, wouldn't it? Stealing crucial evidence from a locked drawer. Let's call the Salem lab."

Ginny got on the phone. The assistant she reached in the photography department started to apologize even before she had finished explaining the problem. They had recently hired some new people; this was not the first complaint. He checked his records, agreed that forty-two prints had been made, and promised to send the missing item by Express Mail. "This is Monday. You should get it by tomorrow afternoon."

"What's so damn important about that picture?" Frank asked.

"I think the twig on the shoe is from a balsam."

"OK, I'm not a forester. Clue me in."

"Balsam isn't a native species." He still looked puzzled. "It doesn't grow here, Frank, unless someone plants it."

Frank took the phone. "I need it right away. Can you have a print ready in two hours? I'll send a courier to pick it up."

He hung up with a pleased smile. "Let me get this straight. Alvarez could have picked up a balsam twig in only two places—his own farm, or Holiday Acres."

Ginny nodded.

"Someone's lying," Frank said. "Either the Alvarez boys or that crew at Holiday Acres."

She closed her eyes, picturing Eduardo and Luis, Felicia, the children, Mrs. Gómez. "Frank," she said, "I don't believe he ever left Galina."

"I'm not that positive, not yet. But it's an assumption we can work from."

She nodded again. "Who are you sending to Salem?"

"You. Get that print; look at it, then give me a call. I'll be waiting right here by the phone."

GINNY CALLED at four o'clock. "I've got the picture. The twig's from a balsam, all right, and it's stuck between the shoe and the black plastic."

"Very good. Have you looked at the shoe itself?"

"Yeah. It's here, along with the mud and the black plastic, but the twig is gone. It could have fallen off when we wrapped the shoe up."

"Well, we're lucky we've got the picture. You're positive there aren't any balsam trees out where the body was?"

"Frank, there isn't a wild balsam west of the Rockies." She paused. "This is what we needed, isn't it? Something connecting Nino's body with Holiday Acres."

"It's what we needed. Congratulations, Deputy."

Frank practically purred as he hung the phone up. Tomorrow he would talk to everyone from Holiday Acres, harvest season or not, and he would finally get some answers.

LATE THAT NIGHT Ginny lay in bed, asleep. The steady rain that had soaked the Coast Range for the last few days was letting up. A light wind blew, tearing holes in the overcast. Stars glimmered and disappeared behind the racing clouds. There was no moon.

The old house creaked gently in the wind, like a ship at sea. The big maple tree was almost bare, its yellow leaves lying in soft mounds where Alice and Rebecca had raked them. A gust of wind rocked the branches and sent rain spattering across the porch roof. Rebecca's rabbit crouched in his hutch. His ears stood straight up, alert to every sound, and his eyes reflected the stray gleams of starlight.

Inside, the sleeping house was alive with tiny noises. Glowing coals shifted and settled in the wood stove. The refrigerator hummed to itself, then fell silent. The clock that had belonged to Dale Trask's grandmother ticked softly in the dining room. Near the ceiling of Ginny's bedroom, a family of mice scratched their way into the insulation, preparing a winter nest. Ginny surfaced briefly from a deep sleep, recognized the faint scrabbling sound, and fell back into dreams.

Suddenly her eyes snapped open. She lay very still, listening. In the kitchen the refrigerator started to hum. Another coal fell in the stove, setting off a cascade of whispers. None of these sounds, familiar as the beat of her own heart, had awakened her. The wind shuffled through the mound of leaves outside, and the mice, temporarily stilled, resumed their burrowing. Ginny drifted back to sleep.

A moment later she was awake again. She sat up, straining to hear through the darkness. Was someone trying the kitchen door? Or was it just the wind, shifting the latched screen door back and forth? Now she thought she heard something from the front door, which they never used, and the faint scrape of someone's foot on the porch. She glanced at the lighted dial of her clock. One A.M.

Careful not to make a noise, Ginny slid open the drawer of her bedside table and took out a flashlight. When Dale was alive, they had kept a revolver there as well. When Dale was alive, they had had a dog, but it had died with him, and Ginny had never felt right about getting another.

She slipped out of bed and padded softly downstairs. She paused by Alice's door and listened for a moment to her sister-in-law's steady breathing. Then she moved to the front door, where she tried the knob—it was firmly locked. She pulled aside the lace curtain and shone her flashlight over the porch. Empty.

Suddenly something moved. She flashed the beam upward and froze. A handlike shape waved from the edge of the roof. She kept the light steady, even though her heart thudded in panic, and saw that it was a clump of sodden leaves, swaying in the wind. She let the curtain drop and turned back into the hall.

The stairs leading up to her and Rebecca's rooms gleamed in the dim light. She paused and listened, but all was quiet upstairs. She moved into the kitchen. A night-light beside the stove cast a pool of yellow on the counter. She tried the kitchen door. The knob turned easily in her hand, and she had another moment of panic. She opened the door and tried the screen. It was firmly latched. No doubt Alice had simply forgotten to lock the back door. Ginny forgot to do it herself, as often as not. She flicked her flashlight on and ran it along the porch, revealing only the empty kindling box and a pile of old newspapers.

She closed the door and locked it, then went around the house, checking the downstairs windows and fastening the latches on the few she found unlocked. As Ginny entered the extra bedroom downstairs, Alice stirred, but did not wake up. Nothing was out of order. Most likely, she had just heard a deer passing below her window. She went back to the kitchen and made a cup of cocoa by the soft gleam of the nightlight.

Just as she sat down at the kitchen table she heard the unmistakable sound of a footstep overhead. It was barely possible that this was Rebecca getting out of bed, but the floor was solid, and they almost never heard her moving around in her room. Ginny grabbed her flashlight, and rushed to the foot of the stairs. She stopped for an instant, long enough to hear a scuffling sound, then pounded up the steps.

"Rebecca! Rebecca!" she shouted.

Suddenly Rebecca screamed. Ginny dashed into the room. Holding her flashlight like a club, she reached for the light switch. The sudden glare made her wince and shield her eyes. Rebecca was sitting up in bed, staring at the half-open window. Wind gusted into the room, puffing the curtains out, then sucking them back

in again. Something scrabbled against the wall outside. Ginny dashed to the window.

A ladder leaned against the outside wall. Ginny
peered into the yard, but could make out nothing definite in the windswept shrubbery.

She turned to Rebecca. "Are you all right?"

Rebecca nodded. "Was someone in my room?"

"It looks that way," Ginny said grimly. She sat down
on the bed and wrapped her arms around Rebecca. A
moment later Alice, finally awakened by the racket,
came into the room. They told her what had happened.

"Oh dear," Alice said. "There've been all those
break-ins at the coast, too, you know."

Ginny's unspoken feeling was that the average burglar would not bother with setting up a ladder and
climbing into a second-story window. The average
burglar, for that matter, was not prowling Tenmile
Road.

"Hadn't we better call the sheriff?" Alice asked.

Ginny nodded. "I'll do that."

"Let's all go downstairs," Alice said. "I don't think
anyone is ready to go back to sleep."

Ginny went over to the window and examined the
ladder. It certainly looked like the one they kept in the
woodshed. Though she knew that evidence should not
be disturbed, she could not bring herself to leave the
ladder there, ready for the intruder to make another
try. She put her palms against the ends and shoved. The

ladder swayed back, paused, then toppled onto the lawn. Ginny pulled the window closed and locked it.

She followed Alice and Rebecca downstairs and went into the living room to call the sheriff's office. The dispatcher could not offer any immediate help. Two deputies were on duty, and both were busy at the other end of the county. She suggested that Ginny ask a neighbor to spend the night.

Ginny had a better idea. She dialed Frank Carver's home number.

Frank's voice was groggy with sleep, but he came quickly alert as Ginny told him what had happened. "You were right to move the ladder," he said. "Safety is always the first concern. Do you have a gun?"

"An old twenty-two in the closet."

"Can you load it without shooting yourself?"

"I think I can manage that," Ginny said drily.

"Load it and put it where you can get it in a hurry. Stay awake, keep the lights on. Don't go outside. I'll be there in an hour."

Rebecca was so keyed up that Ginny was afraid she might stay awake until morning. They made more cocoa, then Ginny read to her until she finally fell asleep in Ginny's bed. Frank arrived shortly afterward. He came in smelling of coffee and tobacco, and seemed to take up the whole kitchen as he shrugged his heavy coat off and hung it on a peg.

"Any more trouble?" he asked.

Ginny shook her head.

"I looked around outside, but didn't see anything. We'll take a closer look tomorrow." He glanced at Ginny and Alice. "I can take over now, if you ladies want to go back to bed."

"You're not staying up, are you?" Ginny asked. "I made up a bed on the couch."

Frank shook his head. "Thanks, but I'm wide awake."

"Let me make you some coffee, then."

Alice had a few words to say about burglars before she went back to her room. When the coffee was ready, Ginny poured a cup for Frank and sat down beside him at the table.

"That ladder came from our woodshed."

Frank nodded.

"There isn't a single item of value in this house."

Frank nodded and swallowed some coffee. "Still, somebody wanted to get in."

"Into Rebecca's room. Frank, I'm scared. What's Rebecca got to do with it?"

Frank set his cup down. "I wondered about that, while I was driving out here. Look, two unusual things have happened in Galina lately. The murder of Alvarez and Danny's visitors. Two unusual events may be a coincidence, or there may be a connection. Three unusual events, and I don't believe in coincidence anymore."

"But why Rebecca? What's she got to do with it?"

He studied her for a moment. "You know Danny Meissner pretty well. If you wanted to make him do something he didn't want to do, how would you go about it?"

She shook her head. "I don't know. Harriet used to be able to finagle him around, but even she hasn't had much luck lately."

"What if you threatened to hurt someone he loves?"

She went suddenly pale. "My God, Frank. You can't mean that. Not my kid."

"Who else? His mother?"

"No. Maybe Susie, but you're right. I believe he'd give in if Rebecca were threatened."

"Well, then, that's my best guess. I've talked to some people I know in LA, and they're keeping an eye out for Danny's visitors. I'm guessing they want something from him—money or information—and he didn't cough up. This is the next step."

Ginny was silent. She looked numbed, her prettiness stripped away by shock. She had looked like that when Frank first met her, after she had found Alvarez. He touched her hand. "They aren't nice people, Ginny. But we can keep them from harming your daughter."

"How? Lock her up somewhere?"

Frank shook his head. "What's Rebecca's schedule tomorrow?" He glanced at the clock. "This morning, rather."

"She catches the school bus at seven thirty, then gets home at three forty-five. She has chores and homework. We'll have dinner, then she'll watch a little television and go to bed."

"OK. Let her go through her usual routine. She should be safe on the bus and at school—they aren't likely to stage a kidnapping in full daylight with dozens of witnesses. Can she stay with a friend after school? Someone in Galina?"

Ginny nodded.

"You'll pick her up there. And I'll come home with the two of you."

"Should we tell her not to mention what happened tonight?"

"Oh, no. Let her talk about a burglar. We want her to act naturally."

Ginny looked up. "You want to use her as bait."

"Can you think of something better?"

"She could go out to the coast with Alice."

"I can't protect her out there. And, Ginny, if they want to, they'll find her, wherever she is."

"You want them to try again."

"I want to stop them, so she'll be safe."

Ginny buried her face in her hands. They were caught in a nightmare, and she was too exhausted to think—couldn't think at all, not where Rebecca's safety was concerned. "I don't know, Frank," she mumbled. "I just don't know."

He gently pulled her hands down. Her eyes were a fine, clear gray, and just as steady as they had been the first time he had seen her. "You've been responsible for Rebecca, all by yourself, for a long time. It's a lot to carry. Let me give you a hand."

She met his gaze. "You think this is the best thing to do?"

"Yes. Ginny, believe me, I'm not going to let anyone hurt your daughter."

TWELVE

By TEN O'CLOCK on Tuesday morning, the four main suspects in the death of Nino Alvarez were at Galina Ranger Station, waiting in four different rooms. The district's field crews had gone out hours before, and the station was quiet. One week had passed since Ginny had found Alvarez's body.

"Everybody's here," said Ginny, looking in through the office doorway.

"Good," said Frank. "All comfortable?"

"Harriet wants to get back to the farm, and Danny's pretty grouchy. I gave them coffee."

"Let's start with Harriet, then Susie, just as we planned."

"Ten-four." Ginny disappeared from the doorway.

Frank leaned back in his chair and rubbed his neck. This was finally beginning to feel like an investigation. The photo Ginny had brought back from Salem was conclusive enough for now. When they went to court, and Frank felt increasingly certain they would, expert witnesses would verify that the bit of greenery was indeed from a balsam fir. The important point to Frank, though, was the twig's placement, caught between the shoe and the scrap of black plastic. The murderer had wrapped the twig in with the victim's body before

hauling it out to the woods. Alvarez had died, Frank
was now convinced, somewhere at Holiday Acres, and
each of the four people who had been there that night
was a suspect.

There was also the matter of last night's intruder.
Very early that morning, when Ginny had gone back to
bed, Frank had made two phone calls. He had arranged with Sheriff Holt to station a deputy in Galina
for the day, with instructions to report immediately any
strangers showing an interest in the school. Then he'd
placed a call to California.

Two men had visited Danny Meissner on Saturday.
On Saturday night Frank had talked to Vern Duval, a
vice and narcotics officer in Los Angeles. Frank and
Vern had worked together in the past, and Vern was
glad to lend a hand. Frank wanted to know who the
men were, who they were working for, and if they had
any known pattern of operation. This morning, at
seven, Vern had given him some answers.

Frank sat up as Ginny ushered Harriet Whittaker
into the office. Ginny picked up her notebook and took
her place in the corner.

Harried looked tired. "How long is this going to
take?"

"That depends on you, Mrs. Whittaker."

"I don't see why you're asking me more questions.
I've had to leave Magda in charge at the farm, and I
don't like it." She glared at Frank, then sank back in
her chair. "Let's get on with it, then."

Exhaustion and tension were pushing her close to the edge. Frank kept his voice low. "What I'd like, Mrs. Whittaker, is to hear, in your own words, everything you did on the evening of October the thirty-first, from about six P.M. on. Take your time, and tell me everything you remember. Even small details can be helpful."

"You must think that was when he died. Let me see. That was Halloween, and Susie was going down to the school to help with the kids' party, so we had dinner early. About six thirty. I think that at six Len and I were sitting on the deck, having a beer. After we ate I cleared the table and got the dishwasher going. That's Susie's job, but she'd left for the party by then."

"So Susie was with you at dinner?"

Harried nodded. "Len, Danny, Susie, and me."

"What time did you finish clearing up?"

"It must have been seven fifteen or so. I got some more coffee and went into the office."

"You were expecting Alvarez, weren't you? Had you set a time?"

"Eight o'clock. I did some paperwork while I was waiting, but he didn't show up. Finally I went to bed."

"You would state, then, that you did *not* drive up to Jackson Ridge later that evening?"

Harriet gave him a considering look. "Was it that night? I guess I did."

"About what time was that?"

She shrugged. "Nine, ten, I don't remember."

"Mrs. Whittaker, you were seen on Jackson Ridge twice that night, once at eight thirty going to the old lookout, again an hour later, going the other way. You were driving the Holiday Acres station wagon. I'd like to know what you were doing out there."

"If you know that much, you probably know I was chasing my scatterbrained daughter."

Frank nodded. "Tell me about it."

"I was in the office, waiting for Nino. A little after eight I heard the front door open and someone come rushing down the hall. I thought it might be Nino, though he would have knocked. I stepped into the hall and Susie almost ran me over. She was extremely upset." Harriet paused. "I've already told you she has emotional problems."

"What was she upset about that night?"

"I suppose I'm going to have to tell you everything." Harriet sighed. "I talked to my lawyer last night, after Ginny called. He told me that if you've turned up evidence connecting the murder to the farm, the best thing I can do is cooperate. Even if I don't like it."

"He gave you good advice." Frank hoped he would never see that lawyer in court. Knowing only that his client was being questioned the second time, he had put his finger on the crucial point. "You saw Susie in the hall?" he prompted.

"That's right. She was upset, she wouldn't tell me why, she just dashed into her room and slammed the door. A few minutes later she dashed out again, ran outside, and I heard her car start. I got the station wagon and took off after her. I wasn't too surprised when she headed for the old lookout. She's always gone up there, ever since she got her driver's license.''

"Did you catch up with her?''

Harriet nodded. "We sat and talked. It's a pretty spot. You can see part of the Neskanie Valley, and there was a full moon.'' She paused, then went on in a dull voice. "Susie told me she'd been having an affair with Nino, and that he had just told her he was married.''

"Did she say she was pregnant?''

The question seemed to throw Harriet a little, just as Frank had hoped it would. "I don't think she knew then.''

"You say he had just told her he was married. So she had seen him that night?''

"Just before I saw her at the house.''

"Where did she meet him?''

Harriet looked up. "I don't know. I didn't ask.''

So that was why Susie had burst into tears when he had wanted to know the last time she had seen Nino. And then she had lied. "Mrs. Whittaker,'' he asked, "did you warn Susie not to tell anyone she had seen Alvarez that night?''

Harried nodded. "When I heard he'd been murdered.''

"Did your daughter kill him?''

Harriet's face suddenly crumpled, and she gave a deep, anguished moan. "Oh, my God, oh, my God.''

Frank waited. Could Susie, rejected, knowing she was pregnant, have killed her lover? Frank believed that every human being was capable of murder, given the right circumstances. That included both an emotionally distraught girl and her overprotective mother.

Ginny pushed a box of tissues toward Harriet, who yanked one out and dabbed at her eyes. She wadded the tissue into a ball and sat quietly, squeezing it in her hand.

"Did Susie kill him?" Frank asked again.

"I don't believe she would. She's never been violent, except toward herself."

"And you, Mrs. Whittaker, did you kill him?"

Harriet's reddened eyes met Frank's. "God knows I wanted to. But no, I didn't."

THEY TOOK A BREAK THEN. Ginny escorted Harriet to the ladies' room, where Harriet bathed her face and put on powder and lipstick. When they got back to the office, Frank had poured coffee. Harriet's hand trembled as she lifted her cup. Ginny pushed hers to one side. She had a feeling they were going to drink a lot of coffee today.

"Let's back up a bit, now," Frank said. "The four of you finished dinner, and you cleared the table. What did the others do at that point?"

Harriet considered. "Well, Susie went out, to the school party, I thought at the time. Danny had some phone calls to make, and Len went out to the equipment shed."

"Did you see any of them again that night?"

"Susie, of course. When we got home I gave her a sedative and put her to bed. Len was in the living room, watching television. I went in and sat with him until eleven, then we said good night and went to bed."

Frank's ears perked up. "Do you and your husband share a bedroom?"

"No. I wanted separate rooms."

Frank nodded. Minerva had insisted on her own room when the girls had moved out. He had not liked it, and he wondered what Len Whittaker thought of the arrangement.

"You didn't see Danny again?"

"Not until breakfast the next morning."

"Do you know if anyone left the house that night, besides you and Susie?"

Harriet shook her head. "I wouldn't hear anyone leave. My room's at the end of the hall, at the far end of the house from the garage."

Frank paused, then changed course. "You said, the last time I talked to you, that Alvarez was a good employee. Hardworking and responsible. You must have trusted him a great deal."

"I did," Harriet said bitterly. "After Wes died I turned some of the farm management over to Danny, but that was a mistake. Nino handled it much better."

"That must have been hard for you to accept, that a hired employee was more competent than your own son."

Harriet sighed. "Neither of my children has been a big success."

"Up until your suspicions about embezzlement, how did you feel about Alvarez?"

"Quite frankly, I wished Danny was more like him. They always seemed to get along, and I hoped some of it would rub off."

"Did you ever have any reason to think Alvarez might be taking things from the farm?"

"No," Harriet said. "That was one of the reasons I trusted him. There's a certain amount of petty theft among the employees, of course. Hard hats go missing, rain gear, rubber boots are a big favorite. We budget for it—it's easier than running tight security. But I'm certain Nino wasn't a thief."

Frank felt certain that Nino had, in fact, taken numerous small items back to Harmony. He saw no point in bringing it up now, though. "You say he got along with Danny. What about the others at Holiday Acres?"

"Everyone seemed to like him. He did a lot of field supervision, of course, working with the hired crews. I know Magda thought the world of him."

"The embezzlement must have come as a shock."

"Not as big a shock as Susie's pregnancy. I still don't believe Nino took that money. But I felt absolutely betrayed that he had slept with my daughter, especially when he hadn't even told us he was married."

"One last question, Mrs. Whittaker. I understand you grow balsam firs at Holiday Acres."

"We've got about five thousand right now."

Frank pushed a piece of paper toward her. "Could you sketch the farm, and show me where they are?"

Harriet took the paper, looking puzzled, and did as he asked. "We've got some here, in the field by the creek, and another acre behind the packing shed. We'll start harvesting them next year."

"So you haven't cut any this season?"

"No. They haven't been doing as well as Wes hoped."

"Have any of your employees worked with them?"

"We sheared in the summer. They were sheared along with all the rest."

Frank nodded, thinking of the cabin Alvarez had lived in, used for storage now. Ginny had pointed out the chaps the shearers wore. A litter of needles and twigs had spilled out as she took a pair down to show him.

"Thanks, Mrs. Whittaker. If you'll just go back to the room you were in before."

"When can I go home?"

"I'll let you know. It shouldn't be long." He got up and saw her to the door, then watched her shuffle down the hall, her shoulders slumped, one foot faintly dragging. For just a moment he felt sorry for Harriet Whittaker. Whatever she might have done or left undone, she was paying a heavy price.

GINNY TURNED TO a clean page in her notebook and gave Susie Meissner an encouraging nod. The girl sat with her hands clasped in her lap, smiling awkwardly.

Her eyes, no longer swollen from tears, showed more confidence than Ginny had ever seen in them before.

"Miss Meissner," Frank said sternly, "when we talked the other day your answers were, shall we say, less than complete. It seems clear now that you did, in fact, see Nino Alvarez on the night he died. I want to know when, and what both of you said and did."

Susie's voice was steady. "I did see him that night. I was afraid to tell you—Mother said that if I did, you might think I'd killed him."

Frank kept his face impassive. "Did you kill him?"

"Of course not."

"Did you meet him that night?"

She nodded. "I drove by the station and left a note in his car. That's how we usually did it."

"Why did you want to see him?"

Susie looked uncomfortable. "I hadn't seen him for over a month, and I had to talk to him."

"Where did you meet?"

"In the old cabin. We usually met there, when he lived at the farm."

"What time was this?"

"About seven thirty."

"And you told him you were pregnant?"

She nodded, then added in a low voice, "I told him I wanted to get married."

"You didn't know, then, that he was already married?"

"No," she said miserably. "I don't know if it would have made any difference if I'd known. Maybe."

"Then what happened?"

"He told me about his family. I got upset. I started screaming."

"What did Alvarez do?"

"Nothing. He just sat there. After I calmed down he tried to talk to me, said he wanted to do something for the baby, but I wouldn't listen. I started crying. I said I never wanted to see him again, and then I ran away." Her hands twisted together in her lap. "I never did see him again, either."

"How long did you spend at the cabin?" Frank asked gently.

"Fifteen or twenty minutes."

"You took your car when you left after dinner?"

She nodded.

"You drove right up to the cabin, then?"

"No. I'd told Mother I was going to help with the party at the school, so I parked at the foot of the driveway and walked to the cabin. There's a path there, around the bottom of the little hill."

"And Alvarez? Did he drive to the cabin?"

"No. He left his car at the foot of the driveway, too. I saw it when I got mine."

"That was before you went back to the house. Why didn't you just walk over to the cabin from the house?"

"Because I had to make Mom think I was going to Galina."

"This place where you left your car, can it be seen from the house?"

She shook her head.

"Now, was it dark when you left the house the first time?"

"After dinner? Oh, yes. It gets dark about six, that time of year."

Frank nodded. Holiday Acres had no streetlights, no neon signs; the moon had been full that night, but covered on and off by clouds. It would have been easy to walk unnoticed almost anywhere on the farm.

"All right," said Frank. "Let's back up a bit. I understand you do the cooking. Did you fix dinner that night?"

She nodded. "We had cupcakes for dessert, with Halloween decorations. I was supposed to take some to the party."

"Who was there for dinner?"

"Well, Mother and Len, of course, and Danny. And me."

"What did the others do after dinner?"

"I don't know. Len said he wanted to look at the new backhoe, but everyone was still at the table when I left."

Frank took her over the wild drive out to Jackson Ridge, confirmed that when they got home Harriet had given her a sedative. Susie had seen no one else until breakfast the next morning.

"Now, Susie," he said, "I know we've been over this, but I need to ask you again about your relationship with Nino Alvarez. When did you first become intimate with him?"

Susie told her story again, with prodding from Frank, but she had little to add to what she had said on Friday. Finally Frank sent her to find her mother, with permission for both of them to go home.

Ginny turned to him. "Do you really think Susie could have done it?"

"It would surprise me, at this point. Though I've been surprised before." He thought for a moment. "I would expect, given the kind of girl Susie is, that if she'd killed Alvarez she would have broken down and confessed before now."

"She has someone to protect."

"Who? Danny? Her mother?"

"The baby," Ginny said.

"Of course." Frank nodded. "She has a future worth living for now, doesn't she?"

THIRTEEN

LEN WHITTAKER settled himself in the chair across from Frank. There was a touch of amusement in his eyes as he surveyed the overcrowded little office. "Sorry we couldn't find a better spot for you," he said.

"We're managing," Frank replied. He waited a moment. "Mr. Whittaker, I'd like a statement of your movements on the night of October thirty-first."

Len grunted. "You ask Harriet and Susie for that, too?"

"I did, and I'll be asking Danny as well."

"Getting things narrowed down?"

"Alvarez was last seen alive at Holiday Acres."

Len raised his eyebrows. "Not at the house. He didn't show up for that appointment with Harriet."

"No, apparently not. Now, your movements for that night?"

"Let me see, Halloween." Len closed his eyes for a moment. "Right, we got the backhoe. See, we were putting in drainage down by the creek. So instead of hiring someone to do it, I rented a backhoe. It arrived that afternoon. OK, so I had dinner with everyone—"

"What time was that?"

"Oh, six, six thirty. The usual dinnertime. Then I went out to look the backhoe over, like I said. After that I checked one of the trucks. Magda told me they'd been having some trouble with it, so I tinkered around a bit under the hood. Must have been out there, oh, a couple of hours. Wouldn't have stayed, of course, if I'd known Alvarez was scheduled to show up.''

"You didn't know your wife was expecting him?"

"Hell, no. I would have had something to say about it if I had. I didn't find out until a few days ago."

"So you got back to the house, when?"

"Almost ten, I guess. Got a beer and sat in front of the tube till Harriet came in. We watched a program, then went to bed."

In their separate bedrooms. "Did Harriet talk to you about Susie at that point?" Frank asked.

"She told me Susie was upset, and that she was worried about her. Didn't go into detail."

"Did you see anyone besides Harriet that evening?"

"Nope."

"And no one but Harriet saw you?"

"Far as I know."

"What did you do the next morning?"

"Let's see, I had breakfast about seven, then took the backhoe out to dig ditches. Went in for lunch about noon, then went back to work until the SO called. That was the California fire." He nodded in Ginny's direction. "Ginny picked me up a little later, and we drove into the station."

"What time was that?"

"Not sure."

"Len called me about two o'clock," Ginny said. "We got to the station at a quarter to three."

Frank nodded. "Anyone out there in the field with you?"

"Not a soul. Damn hot it was, too, for the first day of November."

"All right, Mr. Whittaker. Thanks for going over this." Frank stretched his shoulders and offered Len some coffee. When they were settled back down again, he continued the questioning in a more casual tone.

"You're not from Galina, are you?" he asked.

"No, sir. Grew up in Port Angeles."

"I've been through there," Frank said. "Pretty nice place, out on the Olympic Peninsula."

"Nicer if you've got money." Len sipped his coffee. "My dad worked in a mill all his life, when the work was there, and my mother never did manage to make ends meet."

"Big family?"

"Ten kids. Catholics. Poor-but-clean, wrong-side-of-the-tracks Catholics."

"You've done all right, though."

"Yeah, I guess I have. I was smart enough not to get married right off, for one thing. Then I joined the marines."

"Vietnam?"

"Two years. Supply sergeant. No one shoots at supply sergeants. Were you in the military?"

"Army. Vietnam was a little after my time, though. How did you come to join the Forest Service?"

"It felt like a natural, growing up in a logging town. I took a two-year course on the G.I. Bill, and then got extra points for my military record. Fire control's a lot like the military."

"See your family much?"

"Some. Most of them are still up there, raising a passel of kids, no better off than my folks."

"While you're, what, a full partner at Holiday Acres?"

Len shook his head. "It's in the works. Harriet wanted to give it a year—can't say I blame her, but it does get frustrating. I'll be glad when everything's settled."

"When will that be?"

"January, February at the latest. We run our fiscal year from January to January. Nice for the tax people."

Frank let Len talk a bit more, watching the way he spread himself out in his chair, his rangy arms and legs drooped at odd but comfortable angles. He seemed open enough, willing to talk. Too willing, perhaps? Frank wasn't sure. The average citizen was generally uncomfortable under police questioning. Len was not acting like the average citizen. He was acting, Frank thought, putting it into words for the first time, as though he were part of the investigation. Not directly involved, but an interested professional, watching from the sidelines. Was it possible he did not realize he was a suspect? Frank did not believe that for a moment.

He planted an elbow on his desk and looked at Len. "What do you think about Susie, getting herself knocked up by Alvarez?"

Len stared at him, then narrowed his eyes. Frank smiled to himself. So Harriet hadn't told her husband everything. Pride, perhaps? Or just the stubborn independence that had kept her going after her first husband died. "Were you aware of that fact?"

"Hell, no. I knew she was pregnant." Len shook his head sadly. "Poor Harriet. A lot goes on that she doesn't know about, but this takes the cake."

"You didn't realize, when you were looking into the embezzlement scheme, that Alvarez was seeing your stepdaughter?"

"If I had, I would have put a stop to it, I can tell you that. All the more reason to get rid of him."

"Permanently, perhaps?"

"Now, wait a minute."

"Someone had a reason to remove Alvarez permanently. Was it you?"

Len pursed his lips and studied Frank. "I sure didn't kill him, but I'll admit I didn't like him. Too damn pushy. If someone hadn't stopped him, Harriet would have taken him on as a partner, sooner or later."

"She must have put a lot of trust in him."

"Misplaced trust. I'm not just talking against him because he was a Mexican, I want to make that clear. Doesn't matter to me what race a man is, so long as he's honest. But Alvarez was a thief."

"You're convinced he took that ten thousand dollars."

"It wasn't just the money. A lot of equipment has disappeared over the past few years. I think Alvarez took it."

Frank had to agree with that, and it did make Len's certainty about the embezzled money more understandable. The problem, in Frank's mind, was that Nino had never handled the paperwork end of the business, and embezzlement was almost by definition a paperwork crime. He was beginning to see a way, though, that it could have been done, and if it had happened like that, then both he and Len were right.

LEN WAS GONE. Ginny glanced at the clock. It was almost two. In an hour Rebecca would get out of school and walk with Melinda Forster over to the Forsters' house, just two blocks from the station. At three fifteen Ginny would call Mrs. Forster.

She looked back down at her notes. "I can't believe how much information we're getting. A lot more than the last time we talked to them."

"We know what to ask for now," Frank said. "Most of the time, in a preliminary questioning, you're just testing the water, figuring out where the fish are. In the second go-around you start getting some bites."

"One left," Ginny said. Danny, who felt she had betrayed him, and who might well hold her daughter's safety in his hands.

Frank nodded. "I'll get him."

Danny Meissner came into the little office, glanced quickly at Ginny, and sat down with a sullen look. They might be in for a strike right now, Frank thought, his mind still on fish.

"I'm asking everyone for an account of the evening of October the thirty-first," he said. "Where were you, and what were you doing, from six o'clock on?"

Danny glared at him. "You've taken your sweet time getting around to asking, haven't you?"

Frank lifted an eyebrow.

"I've been stuck in that little room for hours, listening to the secretaries gossip. Why should I talk to you at all?"

Frank almost bit his tongue to keep from pointing out the alternative, a cell in the county jail. "I'm sorry you've had to wait, Mr. Meissner."

"Not that I've got anything to tell you," Danny grumbled.

Frank gave him a curt nod. "Let's go back, then, to your movements on the night of the thirty-first. I understand you had dinner with your family about six?"

"If they say so."

"Mr. Meissner, I am not here to play games. Answer the question yes or no."

"Yes, then. I had dinner with them."

"And after that?"

"I made a few phone calls, and then I went out."

This was new. None of the others had mentioned Danny going out. "Where did you go?"

"To a party."

"You drove?"

"Of course. It was in Longmont."

"Which car did you take?"

"I took my own car, my Volvo."

"Did anyone see you leave?"

Danny shrugged.

"Where was the Volvo parked?"

"In front of the house."

Frank mentally reconstructed the layout of Holiday Acres. Could Len, in the equipment shed, have seen or heard Danny leave? He didn't think so.

"And you drove straight to the party in Longmont?"

"I stopped at the tavern first, for a beer."

"Did you see anyone you knew?"

"Lots of people."

"Their names, please. We'll want to verify that you were there."

"They won't be any help. I was wearing a costume."

"What kind of costume?"

"Batman! It was pretty neat."

"Was anyone else in costume?"

"You bet. They give you a free beer if you show up in costume on Halloween. The place was packed."

Frank groaned inwardly. Didn't any of these people have decent alibis? Susie and Harriet could vouch for each other, but one of Frank's theories was that they had collaborated on the murder. Len had been working on a truck, then watching television. And now this.

"Do you still have the costume?"

"Nope. Rented it from a place in Eugene."

Frank got the address, then pressed Danny for details of the party in Longmont. A fraternity bash, by the sound of it, and he doubted that anyone would be able to vouch for Danny's presence.

"What time did you get home?"

"Not too late, twelve maybe. Everyone else was in bed."

Frank leaned back and studied Danny for a moment. It was clear that he would get nothing but the most grudging cooperation. He let his chair come down with a little thump.

"How did you and Alvarez split the take from the payroll scam?"

Danny's head jerked up. "I don't know what you're talking about."

"I think you do, and I want some answers. Fifty-fifty? Or did you get more?"

Danny glared at him.

"Come on, Danny. Len thinks Alvarez did it, your mother thinks you did. I think neither of you could have pulled it off alone, but together you made a perfect team. Was it your idea? You already knew Alvarez had been walking off with equipment for years. Did you threaten to turn him in? Or was he willing to cooperate without that?"

"You don't know any of that. You're just guessing."

"Your mother won't press charges, so you're safe there. But if you refuse to cooperate now, when the question is murder, I'm going to start wondering what else you and Alvarez were involved in. I'm going to start wondering if you killed him."

"Damn you anyway," Danny snapped. "I didn't kill Nino. He was my friend. I admit the other stuff—we did it together. I handled the bookkeeping, got the checks ready for the old lady to sign, and Nino did the rest. Once he'd cashed a check he gave me half the money."

"You knew he'd been taking equipment, too?"

"Sure, I knew. What did I care? Harriet's always been tight with money, and now that Len's there it's even worse. I didn't care if Nino helped himself now and then."

"I expect you did, too."

"So what if I did? It's a family business, and it's my family."

"Do you know what Alvarez was doing with the equipment?"

Danny shook his head.

"Do you know what he did with his share of the embezzled funds?"

Again Danny shook his head. "Never asked."

"And your share, what happened to it?"

"I spent it."

"On what?"

"On stuff. It's none of your business."

"I'm making it my business fast. Was it for drugs?"

"Some of it, maybe."

"And what else?"

Danny was silent.

Frank leaned forward. "Danny, three days ago you didn't want to tell me about Alfonz Martin's toughs."

Danny's head jerked up.

Frank went on. "Last night someone broke into Rebecca Trask's bedroom. Are Martin's men still around here?"

"I don't know." Danny's voice was defiant, but there was a new uncertainty in his eyes. "What would they want with Rebecca, anyhow?"

Frank lowered his voice. "Danny, if they threatened to hurt Rebecca, would you do whatever it is they want?"

Danny glanced at Ginny, then dropped his gaze to the floor. "They wouldn't do that," he muttered.

"Wrong," Frank said. "They'll do anything they need to. Now, what do they want from you?"

"Money." Danny hesitated. "I went to Vegas a couple of times."

"You lost money gambling?"

"Won some, lost some."

"What else did you spend the money on? Drugs? Girls?"

Danny glared at him. "I don't want to talk about it." He jerked his head in Ginny's direction. "I don't want to talk about it in front of *her*."

Frank turned to look at Ginny, whose face was slowly flushing a vivid scarlet. She kept her eyes on her notebook.

"Mrs. Trask is my deputy," he told Danny. "Even if I asked her to leave, I would immediately tell her everything you said. We'll keep your information as confidential as possible."

Danny looked away from them both, one hand playing nervously with his lower lip. "I went to one of those whorehouses," he mumbled. "The ones on ranches you read about. It cost a lot of money."

"You must have gone more than once," Frank said. "It doesn't cost five thousand dollars."

"Oh, I took some friends along." Danny shrugged and finally looked at Frank, steadfastly ignoring Ginny's presence. "We had a good time."

"I hope so. You sure enough paid for it."

Ginny's pencil scratched once or twice, then fell silent. Frank let the pause lengthen before he spoke again. "What were you doing up on Jackson Ridge the morning after Halloween?"

Danny looked up. "Just poking around."

"Poking around doing what?"

"Look, I was out driving around in the woods, OK? You live with Harriet and Len for a while, and you'll want to get out of the house, too."

"Did you talk to Casey Mullen?"

"The watchman? Yeah, we talked for a minute."

"Where exactly did you go?"

Danny shrugged. "Just tromped around in the woods. Went down to the old lookout."

"Did you see anyone else up there that morning?"

"Just old Mullen."

Frank studied Danny for a moment. "Do you know that your sister's pregnant by Alvarez?"

"No!" Danny's eyes widened. "No kidding! That little turkey buzzard. With Susie! Who'd have guessed?"

"No one, apparently."

"Does Harriet know? I'll bet she's fit to be tied." Danny chuckled appreciatively.

"How do you think your stepfather would take the news?"

"Len?" Danny thought for a moment. "Most likely he'd consider it a personal insult. He's getting real respectable, Len is."

"ALL RIGHT," Frank said when Danny had left. "What's going on here?"

"About what?" Ginny asked.

"Let me guess. Danny's got such a delicate sense of morals that he doesn't want to talk about prostitutes in front of a lady."

Ginny blushed again. "It's more personal than that."

"Well? Let's have it."

"Danny's got a sort of crush on me."

"That's all?"

"No, no it's not." She took a deep breath. "I'm not very proud of this, Frank. About two years ago I slept with Danny a few times."

"Jesus Christ, Ginny, what am I going to do with you?"

"I called it off after a couple of weeks, but Danny's always thought we might get back together."

Frank massaged his forehead with one hand. "Does everyone know this but me?"

"No, thank goodness. I think Harriet guessed. She's never said anything direct about it, but she's dropped hints." Ginny paused. "You've known from the beginning that these people were my friends."

Frank nodded. "I didn't realize how vulnerable it would make you." He had not realized, either, how much he would care.

"You've been personally involved," Ginny said quietly. "When your partner's daughter was killed."

"Of course I was. I'd been on the case for over a year. I knew all the background, all the suspects. Who else was going to do it?" He looked up. "You know what happened?"

"From Maureen."

The story would probably follow him all his life. Frank wished he could feel proud of it, the way other people seemed to think he should. Instead he kept thinking about Paul, locked away just as surely as if he had been convicted of murder.

"Maureen said they did it as a warning."

Frank nodded.

"Those men who are after Danny. Who did you say they were working for?"

"Alfonz Martin. A West Coast gangster. It was just an educated guess."

"Danny knew who you were talking about."

Frank nodded again. "Martin's not a major force out here, not yet. They say he's working on it."

"Can Danny stop him?"

"If he's got the money."

There was a silence. "Are you staying at our house again tonight?" Ginny asked.

Frank responded with a question of his own. "Do you still want to go through with this?"

"I haven't come up with anything better." She glanced at the clock. "School got out ten minutes ago."

"You'd better call Mrs. Forster. Tell her we'll pick Rebecca up about six."

"It's been a long day already."

"Ginny, my dear, it may get much longer before it ends."

FOURTEEN

REBECCA ANSWERED the Forsters' telephone. The girls had arrived there on schedule. She was full of chatter, so that Ginny was on the phone longer than she had expected.

Frank came back into the office just as she hung up. "Everything OK?" he asked.

"Rebecca's fine, and nothing unusual happened at school. But I'm afraid all the excitement is going to her head. She's getting way too much attention."

"You finding Alvarez's body, and now this break-in."

"Plus seeing Bigfoot. Her report's due on Friday." Ginny fell silent and gazed out the window.

"What did you think about the interviews?"

"You know, what struck me was how they have different impressions of Nino. To Harriet he was a responsible son, someone she could lean on. Then he was Susie's lover, Danny's friend and accomplice, and to Len he was an enemy, an interloper. It's almost as though Nino were a mirror, reflecting what each of them wanted to see."

"Or a con artist," Frank said drily. "What was your own impression of him?"

"He was always friendly, but a little reserved. He had a lot of dignity, but he didn't look like the kind of person you'd think of as dignified. He wasn't very tall, you know, not much bigger than me, and he was very nice looking. Big brown eyes with long lashes, wavy black hair, a shy kind of smile."

"You liked him, didn't you?"

She nodded. "So did Rebecca. Rebecca would like anyone who was nice to Susie."

They sat in silence for a moment, then Ginny went on. "I've been trying to imagine how Harriet felt. First Len convinced her that Nino was taking the money and got her to fire him. Then she learned that Danny was involved. Apparently she decided at that point that Nino had been innocent. Innocent of embezzlement, at least. Do you think she knew he was taking stuff home?"

"I doubt it," Frank said. "So there she was, ready to make amends, and what happens? She finds out he's seduced her daughter, that he's been married all along, that he has children. Even worse, he's kept all this secret from her, from Harriet, who thought of herself almost as his mother."

"I'll bet she was furious."

"She's a strong woman. Strong enough to run someone through with one of those shearing knives."

"I've seen her use them, too," Ginny said. "She's good."

"And then Susie helped her dump the body in the woods."

"I guess it could have happened like that."

"Or Susie could have killed him, confessed to Harriet, and they got rid of the body together." Frank was silent for a moment. "I wish we could find that damn car."

"Could we have all the Holiday Acres vehicles searched?" Ginny asked. "If it *was* Harriet and Susie, and they dumped the body that night, they must have taken it up there in either Susie's bug or the station wagon."

"It's a long shot, after all this time, but we might find something."

They were quiet again. "What about Len?" Frank asked.

"He didn't like Nino from the start. Pushy. Somehow I can't see Nino being pushy."

"Ah, but Alvarez never threatened you."

"How did he threaten Len?"

"Just by being there, by being a man Harriet could lean on. Len doesn't want any competition."

"But all he had to do was get Nino fired," Ginny said. "Murder seems a bit extreme."

"He did get him fired. Then Harriet was ready to take him back on."

"But he didn't know that."

"He says he didn't know."

"And he hasn't got an alibi."

"None of them has an alibi that's going to do any good, but Len's is the flimsiest."

"It just doesn't sound like enough of a reason to kill someone," Ginny said. "Though I don't suppose murderers are particularly reasonable."

"Some of them are reasonable, given their premises. I'd vote no on Len, though, because we can't place him near the body. Casey Mullen's quite definite about who was up there that night and the next day."

"So that leaves Danny."

"A difficult young man, Danny Meissner. Very different from his sister."

"I don't know about that," Ginny said. "They've both got a tremendous resentment against their mother, and you can hardly blame them. She's never let them leave home. The difference is that Susie turns it in on herself, and Danny acts it out."

"If Danny were going to kill someone, I'd expect it to be Harriet."

"He's always been trying to get away, to escape," Ginny said. "Harriet keeps a tight leash on both of them."

"Financially, you mean?"

"And emotionally. She's got all a mother's tricks— guilt, martyrdom, the whole show. But yes, Danny always needs money."

"I'm surprised he hasn't tried blackmail," Frank mused. "That seems right up his alley."

"Could he have blackmailed Nino?"

"Perhaps that's how he got him to cooperate with the embezzlement. Then Nino threatened to tell Harriet everything, so Danny got rid of him."

Ginny rubbed her forehead. "Maybe this, maybe that. There are just too many possibilities."

Frank nodded. "Frustrating, isn't it? A jigsaw puzzle with missing pieces. Well, shall we type up those notes of yours?"

"You can type?" she asked in surprise.

"Of course I can type. The question is, can I read your handwriting?"

Most of the district personnel had gone home for the day, so they worked in the front office, Ginny at Maureen's word processor and Frank pounding away on the typewriter. At first he stopped every few minutes to ask about something, but soon he was transcribing almost as fast as she was.

They finished just before six, picked Rebecca up at the Forsters', and reached Ginny's house about seven. Alice had taken advantage of her afternoon off to do some shopping and visit a friend in Longmont. The kitchen was strewn with half-empty grocery bags, and Alice was standing on a chair, looking for a place to store an extra box of cereal.

"Dinner in a few minutes," she said, scrambling down from her perch. "I put some soup on before I left."

Frank made a quick tour of the house while they waited. Everything was as they had left it that morning, with no signs of unwanted visitors. When he got back to the dining room, dinner was on the table.

Over dessert Rebecca told him about the Bigfoot report she and three classmates would be presenting on

Friday. "Did you know that Bigfoots have been seen all over the West, and up in Canada, too?" She set her fork down and launched into her subject. Ginny listened with half an ear, her mind teased by something she had been thinking of early in the day. Something about Bigfoot. She saw again the map she had shown Frank, with the dead-end roads on Jackson Ridge and the old lookout tower.

"Anyway, I told everyone you'd draw us a picture," Rebecca said.

"What?" Ginny looked up.

"Come on, Mom, I told you the other night. We need a picture of Bigfoot. You said you'd help me."

"OK. You help Aunt Alice with the dishes, and I'll get my sketch pad."

When they were alone at the table, Ginny turned to Frank. "Last night, you said there had been two unusual events in Galina. But there's been another one, and it involves Rebecca. She saw Bigfoot."

"She said something about that when I was here for dinner the other night."

Ginny nodded. "She's doing this report for school. But she got interested in Bigfoot because she thinks she saw one. Right out by our creek. And, Frank, it was on Halloween night. The night Nino disappeared."

Frank looked thoughtful. "OK. I think I follow. How far is this house from the spot where you found the body?"

"By car, you have to go out to the Neskanie River, then up Jackson Ridge and around. But if you walk right up the creek, it's a mile, maybe a little more."

"What do you think Rebecca saw that night?"

"To be honest, Frank, at first I didn't think she'd seen anything. She'd been sick, she was running a fever, and she'd been to a costume party that evening— I thought she was having bad dreams."

"You say 'at first.' You must have changed your mind later."

"When Danny heard about it, he came over with Joe Gilmore, Magda's husband—he's really into Bigfoot—and they looked around. They were both convinced that something big had been in the area."

"Bigfoot?"

"They certainly hoped so. At that point I figured it was a bear. We don't have a lot of them around here, but I have seen one or two on the road. I didn't say anything. Rebecca was all wired up about her report, and I didn't want to discourage her."

"So she may have seen the murderer disposing of the body."

Ginny nodded. "I'll get my sketch pad."

THEY SAT IN the living room, in front of the fireplace. The lamp beside the couch cast a bright spot of light over Ginny's shoulder. Rebecca sat beside her, eyes closed, her forehead furrowed with the effort of remembering. Frank was in an overstuffed chair in a corner, almost lost in the shadows, and Alice was knitting on the other side of the room.

Ginny held her pencil over her sketch pad, moving it in sweeping arcs to loosen up her hand. In the fireplace a flame leaped, sputtered briefly, and sank back. Ginny's pencil slowed and hung poised over the blank paper.

Rebecca began the game. "I see something with my magic eye."

Ginny gave the response. "Tell me, Rebecca, what you see."

"Big," Rebecca said. "Really big."

Ginny's hand dropped to the paper. A large, faintly human form took shape under her pencil.

"Short legs," Rebecca murmured. "And big shoulders. Way too big."

Ginny's pencil hesitated, then moved again. Now she could almost see it herself, a shadowy form moving through the deeper shadows of brush and trees. Clouds scudded across the sky, and the moon shone fitfully down on the windblown hills. The creature disappeared into the darkness, then was suddenly picked out in a patch of moonlight, very still, erect, head cocked to one side as though listening.

Frank got up and silently crossed the room to stand behind the couch. Ginny and Rebecca, absorbed in their shared vision, worked on, oblivious of his presence. The creature taking shape beneath Ginny's moving pencil was like nothing Frank had ever seen. A small, rounded head rested directly on oversize shoulders. The arms were raised and curled in close to the body, while the legs disappeared into some sketchily indicated brush.

Ginny added a few details, then laid her pencil down. Rebecca's eyes opened. She turned to look at the drawing.

"That's it," she whispered. "That's just what it looked like."

Ginny took a deep breath and let it out. "You can use this for your report?"

"You bet," Rebecca said. "It's supposed to be our own work, but I can copy this." She looked again at the drawing. "That's great, Mom."

"Yeah," Ginny said. "It's not bad at all."

AN HOUR LATER, when Rebecca had gone up to bed, Ginny spread the drawing out on the dining-room table. She and Frank stood together, studying it.

"It's not a bear," Ginny finally said.

"It's not a Bigfoot, either," Frank added. "It's a human being carrying something on its shoulders."

"Something big."

"Alvarez's body. Do you think Rebecca realizes what she saw?"

Ginny shook her head. "Not yet. All she can think of right now is Bigfoot. But sooner or later she'll start to wonder."

She was standing very close. Frank lifted his arm, hesitated, then slipped it over her shoulders. She shifted her weight slightly, just enough to rest her head against him. Her hair, smelling faintly of soap, tickled his nose.

If she had been his daughter, he would have leaned over and kissed her on the forehead, right where her dark hair came down in a little peak. Should he do it anyway? Before he could gather enough courage for the attempt, she sighed and pulled away.

"Well, I guess I'd better fix a bed for you. I'm sorry the couch is so short."

"It's fine," Frank said. "Don't worry about it."

THE NESKANIE VALLEY lay shrouded in a heavy fog as Magda Gilmore, the Holiday Acres crew leader, drove up to the Christmas tree farm early on Wednesday morning. As usual, she was the first one there. The others would be in by eight. It was still dark when she parked her car and switched the headlights off. The kitchen windows up at the house showed yellow through the fog, and the big lamp mounted on the garage roof gave off a dim but steady glow.

Magda unlocked the door to the packing shed, her keys jingling cold and metallic in the muffling fog. Later she would push back the big sliding doors, leaving one side of the building open, and perhaps fire up the wood stove in the back room. She switched the light on and stood for a moment, looking over the empty tables, the tree baler, the litter of twigs and needles covering the floor. She would sweep up first, then have a cup of coffee from her thermos before the others arrived.

She opened the door to the back room, humming a
Christmas carol under her breath. As she reached for
a broom, something in the corner moved. She froze,
then slowly backed out of the darkened room, keeping
her eyes on the gruesome shape swaying gently among
the shadows.

"Mother of God," she murmured. She stood outside the door, listening, but no sound came from the
back room. She crossed herself, something she had not
done for many years, and wished that for just once she
had not been the first to arrive.

Whatever it was, she had seen worse as a child during the war. Holding the broom in front of her like a
weapon, she pushed the door open and turned the light
on. The dangling body swayed gently, rotating in the
draft from the open door. The face turning slowly toward Magda, with an expression of calm in spite of the
protruding tongue, was Danny Meissner's.

FIFTEEN

GINNY CLUTCHED THE SEAT and leaned forward in the truck as Frank took the turn into Holiday Acres. She peered through the fog, her stomach tight with apprehension. Half an hour ago she had been plugging in the coffeepot at the ranger station, her mind still foggy with sleep. When the phone started ringing, Frank answered it. A minute later he stood in the door, his coat already on. "That was Sheriff Holt," he said. Then he told her about Danny.

The fog thinned as they reached the top of the little hill. Ahead of them the Holiday Acres house and outbuildings loomed indistinctly in the gray pall. Suddenly they were at the packing shed, where Harriet, Len, and Magda waited like silent wraiths. Streamers of fog drifted through the square of light from the open doorway.

Magda stepped forward as Frank and Ginny got out of the truck. She beckoned, and they followed her inside. Ginny's heart was pounding as they approached the storeroom. Magda pulled the door open to reveal Danny's body, turning slowly toward them.

"My God," Ginny murmured. She bit her lip as the shock and grief stabbed down through her like a knife. She had known what they would see, but she also knew that no one was ever truly prepared to look death in the face. She turned away, her shoulders shaking.

A moment later she looked up and found Frank watching her.

"You OK?" he asked in a soft voice.

She nodded.

"Come on, then," he said, turning gruff. "We've got work to do."

By midafternoon the police team from Longmont was ready to pack up. The fog had burned off about eleven, revealing a high, pale sun in a clear sky. A soft breeze blew in from the coast, so that a few of the investigators had taken off their jackets. All their gear was stowed away, the evidence they had collected sealed in bags and boxes, labeled and ready for the crime lab. Danny's body had been removed earlier and was now waiting in the autopsy room at St. Ben's. Doc Jarvis had promised to call Frank about six, with the preliminary results.

Frank was doing his best to keep an open mind. Murder or suicide? Murderers rarely killed by hanging, suicides often. The body had been strung from an easily accessible beam, on a rope identical to a dozen others stored in the shed. There was no note, no sign of a struggle, just a tipped-over chair near Danny's dangling feet.

"I thought suicides always left a note," Ginny said.

Frank shook his head. "Some do, some don't." He studied her for a moment, then turned away before she could notice his concern. She was doing all right. Her initial shock had been swept away by the mass of details needing immediate attention. A few times that morning he had found her staring absently into space, and once he had seen tears on her cheeks, but she had quickly wiped them away and gone back to work.

At least one of the day's events had been a great cause of relief to them both. Shortly before noon Frank had gotten a phone call from Los Angeles. The two men who had paid Danny a visit on Saturday had been picked up in California. The trip to Galina had come up as part of their alibi in an unrelated investigation. Frank's contact verified that they had not been in Oregon since yesterday morning.

"One of them could still have been in Rebecca's room on Monday night," Ginny pointed out.

"But they aren't here now," Frank said, "and with Danny dead they have no further reason to go after Rebecca."

The body had been removed shortly afterward, and since then Ginny had seemed more and more like her usual self.

Frank's guess was that Danny's death was suicide. Danny was the prime suspect in the murder of Nino Alvarez. He had realized this and guessed that he would soon be arrested. That, together with the threat from Alfonz Martin, was enough to make him decide to step out now.

No doubt there were contributing factors: a desire to hurt his family, or perhaps, plausibly enough, a desire to spare them the trauma of a murder trial. Given what he knew of Danny, Frank did not believe this, but it was possible. When he questioned them that afternoon in Harriet's office, the family seemed convinced, too, that Danny had killed himself.

"Had he ever attempted suicide?" Frank asked.

"No," Harriet said tearfully. "But Susie has."

"So you think Danny might have?"

"They're so much alike. Susie's psychologist always said they were two sides of the same coin."

Frank considered this. "Did Susie's psychologist ever see Danny?"

"Twice." Harriet wiped her eyes and twisted the handkerchief between her hands. "She saw everyone in the family at the beginning of Susie's therapy."

"Was this therapy related to suicide?"

Harriet nodded. "It was after Susie took all those sleeping pills." She began to cry again, and Len, standing beside her chair, laid a protective arm around her shoulders.

Frank got the name and address of the therapist. She might not talk to him, claiming patient confidentiality, but that would not stop him from asking.

The call from Doc Jarvis came sooner than he had expected. "I'm afraid I've got bad news, Frank," Jarvis said. "Danny Meissner was strangled before someone slipped that rope around his neck."

"SO HE PROBABLY DID NOT kill Alvarez," Frank concluded. "But my guess is that he knew who did."

"Why didn't he tell us, then?" Ginny asked.

Frank shook his head. "There must have been something in it for him. We know he needed money. Is it possible he was trying to blackmail the murderer?"

"That leaves the other three, then."

"Yep," Frank said. "That leaves the other three."

That night, working in Harriet's office, they questioned everyone again without learning anything helpful. At dinner on Tuesday the family had discussed the lengthy interrogations Frank had put them through that day. They had realized, by then, that he suspected someone at Holiday Acres, and the conversation had not been comfortable. One by one they had gone to their rooms, Harriet last, at about ten, after spending an hour in her office. All claimed to have heard or seen none of the others until breakfast the next morning. No one had missed Danny, who usually slept in, until Magda had burst into the kitchen shortly after seven to announce her discovery.

"Absolutely useless," Frank said, after the last of them had gone. "Is it possible they're all in it together?"

"It's hard to imagine," Ginny said. "But then, I can't imagine killing someone in your own family."

"Twenty percent of intentional homicides are perpetrated by members of the victim's family," Frank said gloomily. "That's a quote."

"Oh." Ginny found this piece of information so depressing that she could think of nothing else to say.

THE HARDEST THING about Danny's death was talking to Rebecca. She had already heard many of the details by the time Ginny got home that night. Frank had not released the information that Danny's death was a homicide—as far as Galina knew, he had taken his own life, probably because he was guilty of murder and could see no way out.

"Well, I don't think he killed Nino," Rebecca said. "They were friends." Then she burst into tears.

At bedtime she asked if she could sleep with Ginny, a request she had not made for years. Ginny tucked her into the big double bed and stayed to talk to her for a few minutes.

"Did you see Susie?" Rebecca asked. "How was she?"

"Upset, crying. She took it pretty hard."

"Poor Susie," Rebecca murmured. "Danny wasn't always nice to her, but she really loved him."

"I know," Ginny said. "You loved him too, didn't you?"

"When I was little, I did. Then he was gone a lot. But I guess that didn't matter to Susie."

Ginny stroked Rebecca's hair away from her forehead and kissed her nose. "You could call her tomorrow. Just tell her you're sorry about Danny, and you're thinking of her."

"OK. I'll do that. Good night, Mom."

She was still asleep when Ginny got up in the morning. Frank had spent the night at his own house in Longmont—all that remained of his presence was a

pair of sheets in the laundry and a noticeable dent in
the couch. Ginny ate a bowl of cereal, added some
wood to the fire, and drove to Galina through a steady
downpour. School would let out for Christmas vacation next week, and she worried about how much
longer she could impose on Alice. In a way, the dead-
line handed down by the regional office was a relief.
Whether they pinned down the murderer or not, after
Christmas she would, as Frank said, be back on the
radio, talking to idiots.

But if they did not pin the murderer, she thought
grimly, she was not going to be happy about it. She was
still considering the suspects when she pulled into the
district compound and parked beside Frank's rig. He
had never beaten her in before. She laid a hand on the
hood; still warm, so he had not been there long.

"Any news?" she asked as she walked in.

Frank shook his head. "I called the crime lab and
talked to some guy who told me to keep my shirt on.
They'll call us back about noon."

Maureen Evans was running Dispatch from the front
desk. Her voice murmured from the radio, laughing
pleasantly as she signed on and off. There was really
very little for Ginny to do. Until they heard from the
crime lab, they were at a dead end. Frank was counting, she knew, on getting something, anything—hair,
fibers, a bit of soil—that would connect Danny's body
with one of the suspects.

Frank handed her a sheaf of papers. "Here's our
report on Danny Meissner's death. Get it typed up, and

then you can run it in to the SO for Hunsaker. While you're in town, stop at the hospital and pick up a copy of the autopsy report from Doc Jarvis. I'll call and let him know you're coming."

An hour later Ginny was on her way to Longmont, a copy of the typed report lying on the seat beside her. If she had put it in the mail, Hunsaker would have gotten it the next day, which would have been soon enough, but her guess was that Frank wanted to be alone for a while. She did not really mind—anything was better than sitting around the office, fretting because there was nothing to do.

She handed the report over to Hunsaker's secretary, stopped to talk with a friend in Engineering, then went on to the hospital. As she started back to Galina, the rain turned to a misty drizzle. She took a different route, for variety, and after a few miles was stopped by a flagger. A road maintenance crew was at work on a small slide caused by the heavy rain. As she waited in line with half a dozen other cars, Ginny watched a cat shove dirt around, while behind it a backhoe ate away at the embankment, digging a hole big enough to park a car in.

Big enough to hide a car in. Of course. Nino's car was not rusting away below a cliff along the coast. It was buried somewhere at Holiday Acres.

FRANK STARED GLOOMILY at the papers littering his desk. It was well past lunchtime, and people were drifting toward the employee lounge for afternoon coffee. Frank was thinking he might join them when Ginny hurried through the door. Her hair was more mussed than usual, and her eyes were bright. She came to stop in front of the desk.

"I know where Nino's car is."

Frank raised an eyebrow. "Well, then, I guess you'd better tell me."

She did, in detail.

"I'll be damned," Frank said. "It could have happened like that. But how was Alvarez involved? And why kill him?"

"I don't know," Ginny said. "But I'll bet Maureen Evans does."

"Maureen?"

Ginny nodded, remembering the hand she had glimpsed slipping across Maureen's shoulder a few days ago. "You get her in here, Frank, and you ask her what's been going on."

They talked for a couple more minutes, then Ginny went down to the front desk. Maureen was on the telephone. She glanced up at Ginny and went back to her conversation. Finally she hung up.

"Hi, Ginny. What's going on?"

"Frank Carver wants to talk to you."

"Again? I still don't remember the name of the guy who kept calling for Nino. Can't you just tell him that?"

"Come tell him yourself."

Maureen was not happy about it, but she stepped into the mail room to ask someone to cover the desk.

Ginny followed her down the hall to Dispatch, watching her pink skirt sway with the movement of her hips. Maureen turned just before they reached the door, gave Ginny a troubled look, then went in.

Frank leaned back and watched her as she settled into the chair across from him. Her honey-colored hair was piled on top of her head today, making her look older, and for the first time he noticed crow's-feet at the corners of her eyes. She smiled politely.

Frank set his elbow on the desk with a little thump. "Mrs. Evans, what exactly is the nature of your relationship with Len Whittaker?"

Maureen's smile vanished. "He's my boss while I'm filling in for Ginny."

"Do you ever see him outside of work?"

"Occasionally." Maureen's gaze was steady. "Galina's a pretty small place. We run into each other now and then."

"Do you ever arrange to run into each other?"

"I'm not sure this is any of your business."

Frank leaned forward. "What if I told you that you and Len Whittaker have been seen together in, shall we say, compromising circumstances? More than once, and by more than one person."

"You'd be lying. No one's seen us together."

"I think you're lying, right now. I also think you know something about Alvarez's death. I'm sure you've heard the term *accessory*." He watched closely, but Maureen's expression did not change. Could Ginny be mistaken? He pushed on. "I'd hate to see you go to prison, Maureen. Now's your chance to talk."

"Who says they saw us together?" She gave Ginny a quick, defiant glance. "Was it you? Just because you don't like Len touching you, you think it means something special?"

"Does it mean something special?" Frank asked.

Maureen glared at him. "She thinks she's too good for Len, but then she went and slept with Danny Meissner. Probably thinks she's too good for you, too."

Frank carefully avoided looking at Ginny. "Mrs. Evans," he said, keeping his voice under control, "we are talking about you. We are talking about your affair with Len Whittaker."

"Well, what about it?" she said flatly.

Frank relaxed just a bit. Ginny had been right, but she was paying for it. "How long have you been seeing him?"

"Over a year."

It had started, then, before Len's marriage to Harriet, and apparently was still going on. Before he could ask another question, Maureen asked one of her own.

"Did Danny really kill himself?"

"He was found hanging at the end of a rope. That usually indicates suicide."

She relaxed slightly. Frank leaned forward. "I think someone killed him. Probably the same person who killed Alvarez."

Maureen's head jerked up, and for the first time he saw fear in her eyes.

"Alvarez knew about you and Len, didn't he?"

She nodded slowly. "He caught us together one night, out behind the warehouse." Maureen glanced out the window at the equipment warehouse. Beyond it was the old bunkhouse, where Alvarez had stayed.

"When was this?"

"Last summer, early August I guess."

"And three months later Alvarez was dead. Think about it, Maureen. Two people have died. So far."

Maureen suddenly shivered. "OK, OK." She took a breath. "I didn't care about Nino seeing us. I was tired of sneaking around, always pretending like we didn't know each other. But Len cared. He cared a lot."

"Because of Harriet?"

She nodded. "He figured it would be the end of everything if she found out."

No partnership, no early retirement, no chance to be his own boss and run his own show.

"What happened then?"

"A few weeks later Len told me someone was trying to get money out of him. He wanted to know if anyone knew about us. Well, I hadn't told anyone, and I said so. So he said it must be Alvarez."

She paused. "I didn't think any more about it, until Nino's body turned up. But then I started wondering." She looked at Ginny. "Remember when your daughter saw that Bigfoot?"

Ginny nodded.

"Well, Len thought that was the funniest thing, and he thought it was even funnier when Danny tried to track it down. He said that was just like Danny, off on a wild-goose chase. I don't care if there's a Bigfoot or not, but Len was so snotty about it I asked him how he could be sure. He just smiled and said he'd been out there and he knew."

She sighed. "I didn't think any more about that, either, until you started asking about that night. We'd had a date, and Len stood me up. It was the first time he ever tried that, and I was pretty ticked off." She shrugged. "Well, it fits together, doesn't it?"

Frank nodded. Maureen had more between her ears than he had given her credit for. "You've waited a long time to say anything."

Maureen looked down at her hands. "I didn't care."

Frank stared at her in astonishment.

"It was all too much trouble," she said defiantly. "I just didn't care." She lowered her voice. "Now Danny's dead too, and I'm afraid."

A moment later someone tapped on the office door. Ginny got up and opened it to reveal Alice Trask, shaking rain off her umbrella.

Ginny stepped into the hall. "Alice! What are you doing here? Is Rebecca with you?"

"I'm just on my way into town to do some shopping. I couldn't get through on the phone, so I came by to tell you. Rebecca's up at Holiday Acres."

"What's she doing up there?"

"Len called about an hour ago to ask if she could spend the afternoon with Susie. I guess the poor girl's just miserable, and he thought she might like some company."

Frank was suddenly standing in the doorway, just behind Ginny. "How long has she been there?" he demanded.

"Well, I dropped her off on my way in, so maybe half an hour. I haven't done something wrong, have I?"

"Let's hope not." Frank moved to the door, with Ginny right behind him. Alice and Maureen stood openmouthed as they ran for the truck. They tumbled in and sped past on their way out of the parking lot, red lights flashing through the thin rain.

"IT WAS Len in Rebecca's room that night, wasn't it?" Ginny said, hanging on to her seat as they took the first sharp turn out of Galina.

Frank nodded grimly. "Most likely. And I thought she was safe, once Danny was out of the picture." He grabbed the radio and called the sheriff's office. Reception was poor, but he managed to explain the situation.

"We're on our way," Holt responded. "ETA thirty minutes."

"I hope they're not late," Frank muttered, skidding the truck around another turn. "Now, tell me again about Alvarez's car."

Ginny swallowed. "When I was there that afternoon, the day after Nino died, Len had been running
the new backhoe." She was amazed to find that she
could talk, even with fear pounding at the back of her
head.

"Digging drainage ditches," Frank said, remembering Whittaker's statement. "I'll grant he could have
buried the car. He certainly meant it to look as though
Alvarez had taken off. But I don't understand about
the body. Why did he haul it all the way up the creek
and then not bury it? He must have realized someone
would find it sooner or later."

Ginny shook her head. "He'd thought of that. He
left it in the Cripple Elk unit, the one we were scheduled to burn on Monday. And then, when he knew he
wasn't going to be here, he told me to cancel the burn.
See, he wanted to be in charge when we torched it, to
make sure the body was destroyed."

"But that area *had* been burned."

"We did it later that week, with a helicopter. Len was
still in California." She saw the helicopter again, trailing drops of fire. Then it had veered in a sudden updraft, Ducks swearing over the radio as flames leaped
up from the burning slash. A goddamn funeral pyre,
he had called it, and so it had been intended.

"Len inspected the burn first thing when he got
back," Ginny said. "Remember Sheriff Holt saying
that coyotes had gotten to the body? I'll bet they'd
dragged it away before we got around to burning. Then
when Len went down there, he didn't find anything, so

he figured the body had gone up in smoke, just like he'd planned.''

Frank nodded. ''It fits, just like Maureen's story fits. Once we find the car, we'll have him.''

The harvest operation was in full swing at Holiday Acres, in spite of Harriet's and Susie's grief. Out in the fields crews were cutting Christmas trees and piling them into a cargo net for the helicopter. Ducks Wilson was flying again, after being grounded all morning by the heavy rain. He shuttled back and forth between the fields and the packing shed, picking up trees and dropping them for Magda's crew to bale and tag. Every few hours another loaded truck left the farm, headed for a wholesaler in California.

Frank pulled to a stop beside the packing shed. As they jumped out of the truck, their ears were assailed by a cacophony of noise. The baling machine roared away as a woman in rain gear fed trees into it, but even that was almost drowned out by the racket from the helicopter hovering nearby, ready to drop another load of trees.

Ginny's first thought was for her daughter. She scanned the women in the packing shed, making sure neither Rebecca nor Susie was there, then hurried to the house. Susie could usually be found in the kitchen around mealtime.

Frank wanted Len Whittaker, and he wanted him immediately. He went up to Magda and cupped his hand beside her ear.

''Where's Len?'' he shouted.

Magda glanced around the loading area and gave an expressive shrug. Frank walked quickly past the big truck, half-filled with baled trees, and out onto the open lawn in front of the house. From there he watched Ducks gently lower the cargo net. As it touched the ground, two men ran out and unhooked it from the cable dangling beneath the helicopter. Ducks waved his hand, lifted the ship up into the air, and headed back for another load.

From his vantage point on the lawn, Frank could see most of the Holiday Acres operation. The damn rain gear everyone wore, though, made it impossible for him to tell one person from another. He was just about to turn away and try at the house when he caught sight of Rebecca, standing on a little rise between the packing shed and the road, talking to someone. Her dark hair was plastered to her head by the rain, and she was wearing a bright yellow slicker. Even if she had been yelling, Frank could not have heard her over the racket of the returning helicopter. The person she was talking to, face hidden by a hard hat, was holding a radio. The figure moved, and Frank realized it was Len Whittaker.

At that moment the sheriff's car bumped across the driveway and came to a stop beside Frank's rig. Holt and Deputy Wilcox jumped out. Frank waved his arm frantically. Just as they caught sight of him, Ginny burst out of the kitchen and raced across the lawn, headed for Rebecca.

Len, apparently still unaware of their presence, kept the radio up to his mouth. Ginny knew he was guiding Ducks's helicopter, just as he did on the slash burns. Ducks veered in the air and moved toward the drop point, the loaded cargo net swinging heavily beneath the ship.

Rebecca broke away from Len and rushed down the little hill. She tripped a few yards from the drop point and lay still, her yellow slicker gleaming brightly against the mud. The *whup-whup-whup* of the helicopter pounded in Ginny's ears like the background of a nightmare. She ran toward Rebecca. Her feet slid in the mud, and her breath tore through her throat in ragged gasps. She reached the gravel road, crossed the drop point, and flung herself on her daughter. The sky was filled with noise and flashing rotors. Someone grabbed her arm and tried to pull her away. She screamed. Suddenly Frank Carver was there, wrapping his arms around both her and Rebecca. He threw his body over them just as Ducks, confused by all the activity and unable to see the running figures beneath him, followed Len's orders and released the cargo net, letting half a ton of Christmas trees hit the ground.

EPILOGUE

GINNY MOANED AND STIRRED as a splitting headache forced her into consciousness. A harsh, white glare filled her eyes, seeping through the closed lids. There was something she needed to do, something urgent. Pain hammered away inside her skull. Then the dark, anesthetic tide rose again, and she gratefully let it carry her away, without discovering what she was supposed to be so concerned about.

A few hours later she woke again. The pain had receded to a dull thumping somewhere in the back of her head, and the white glare was gone, though her eyelids felt glued shut. Now she became aware of pain in other parts of her body as well. She tentatively moved a few fingers, then one hand. The other arm refused to respond. She moved her toes, but when she tried to pull her knees up, a great pain rippled across her stomach. She relaxed her legs and worked on getting her eyes open.

She was in a hospital room, next to a window with the shades pulled. The other bed was empty. Her right arm, lying on top of the sheet, was in a cast. She closed her eyes again and rested.

She came out of her doze to find a nurse bent over her, examining the cast. She was older, with gray hair tucked up under a white cap, and she smiled when she saw Ginny's open eyes.

"Hello there. It's about time you woke up."

Ginny moved her swollen tongue inside a mouth that felt like it was stuffed with cotton. She managed a grunt.

"You're at St. Benedict's, in Longmont," the nurse said. "I'm supposed to tell you that your daughter is all right."

That was it, then, the thing she had been trying to remember. Ginny nodded, as far as the stiffness in her neck would allow.

"You were in a farm accident," the nurse said, pouring some water into a glass. "You've been here since yesterday afternoon, and your arm is broken in two places. You've got a lot of bruises, too, but the doctor expects you to live through it. Here's some water. Your mouth must feel awful after the anesthesia."

She held the glass up to Ginny's lips. Ginny took a few sips, dropped her head back on the pillow, closed her eyes, and slept.

When she woke again, a doctor came in to explain that the pain across her stomach and her stiff neck were from bruises. She was lucky her back wasn't broken, he added; she would be in the hospital for another week. Then a different nurse, quite young and full of friendly chatter, helped her into a wheelchair and took her upstairs to the children's wing, where she sat for half an hour watching Rebecca sleep peacefully under sedation.

Rebecca had a mild concussion, but Ginny's and Frank's bodies had cushioned her from worse injuries. She would be up and walking the next day, the nurse said. She promised to bring her to Ginny's room for breakfast.

Ginny's mind was clearer now, and she had had time to think while sitting with Rebecca. She looked up. "What about Frank Carver?"

The nurse smiled. "He's here, too. In fact, I think he might be waiting for you."

She wheeled Ginny back to her room. Frank was there, sitting beside the empty bed, the small bald spot at the back of his head giving him an oddly vulnerable appearance. Beneath the hospital gown, she glimpsed bandages wrapped around his chest.

"Hey, Deputy." He turned toward her, and winced with pain. "How you doing?"

"Still here. What about you?"

"Broken ribs," he said ruefully. "I'm not supposed to be sitting up."

The nurse helped Ginny into bed and asked if she wanted any dinner. Ginny's stomach was still a little queasy, but definitely empty.

"Rice pudding," the nurse suggested. "It's not bad, either."

Frank had a cup of coffee while she ate. "Not as good as yours," he said.

Ginny's first taste of food awakened a ravenous appetite. She finished the pudding, swallowed some juice, and settled back in the bed. "What happened?"

"Len almost got you killed is what happened."

"He was trying for Rebecca."

Frank nodded. "I talked to her for a few minutes this morning. That is one spunky kid. She was chewing Len out because he'd yelled at Susie that morning."

"He got her out there on purpose," Ginny said. "He planned to kill her. We should have told them more, Frank. We should have told Alice to keep Rebecca away from Holiday Acres."

Frank nodded. "Perhaps we should have."

"Where's Len now?"

"In the county jail," Frank said with satisfaction. "Holt and Wilcox grabbed him right away. They were out at the farm this morning with a metal detector, and this afternoon they started digging. The car's there, all right, though they don't have it out yet."

"Has Len said anything?"

"Nope. He's got a lawyer and he's not talking. But we'll get him, don't you worry. The lab found bits of skin and some cloth fibers under Danny's fingernails. Len has fresh scratches on both wrists. With any luck, too, we'll find something in Alvarez's car. Len must have been inside it at least once, to drive it into the field. Wouldn't surprise me if he used it to dump the body, too."

He paused. "By the way, remember that missing photograph?"

"Len had keys to the desk."

Frank nodded. "Never be able to prove it, of course. Hell, he must have known every move we made. All he had to do was read the daily diaries."

"He asked me about the investigation, too, when he did my performance rating." She paused. "You still think it was blackmail?"

"Positive," Frank said, "though if Len doesn't talk we may not be able to prove it. The way I see it, Alvarez told Danny about finding Len and Maureen together, and the two of them set up the blackmail scheme. Len might not have guessed that Danny was involved and figured he was safe once Alvarez was dead. Then Danny made the mistake of trying it again, or even worse, threatening to turn Len in for murder."

"But finally Maureen got frightened, too."

"She knew some of it, guessed some more, but just didn't bother to put it together." He shook his head. "It's hard to picture, isn't it?"

"Maureen's pretty self-centered," said Ginny. "Maybe no more than the rest of us, but she doesn't bother to hide it."

"And too lazy to think, even though she's got the equipment."

"This must be terrible for Harriet."

Frank nodded. "It's going to get worse. I don't think she knows about Maureen yet."

"And Susie? How's she doing?"

"Holt said she was out there watching them dig up the car. When they finally got a fender clear and could see the orange color, she started crying and went back to the house."

"Poor Susie," Ginny murmured. She closed her eyes and lay back on the pillows.

"Getting tired?"

She nodded. "Frank, why didn't you go for Len?"

"Holt and Wilcox were there. They got him."

She opened her eyes. "It must have made a difference, you pushing us down before Ducks dropped those trees." She fell silent, not knowing what to say.

"Well, we're all here, aren't we? That's what counts."

She nodded. "That's what counts. I guess that's it, then? You'll go back to the SO and I'll be back in Dispatch. With a new boss."

"If that's what you want."

She looked up. "What's that supposed to mean?"

"Well, I could recommend to Hunsaker that you go for the full law enforcement training. If you want to, that is."

"Me?"

"You'd be good at it, Ginny," he said earnestly. "You've got a way of getting into other people's heads—I mean, understanding how they think. Well, anyway..." he said, trailing off. "It's something to consider."

Ginny nodded. She would have a lot to consider in the next week. Frank's idea wasn't half bad. She wouldn't mind going to school again, and she rather liked the idea of a real career.

"Well." Frank got up. "I guess that's enough for now. I'll come by in the morning, if that's OK."

"Of course it's OK."

"All right, then." He got up, winced, then leaned gingerly over the bed and kissed her squarely on the mouth. When he stood up again, his face was flushed, but he was smiling. "See you later," he said, and left the room.

The young nurse came in a few minutes later to help Ginny get ready for bed. "He seems like a nice man," she said. "Not your father, though. An uncle?"

Ginny smiled. "Oh, come on," she said. "He's not that old."

B. M. GILL
the Fifth Rapunzel

First Time in Paperback

AN
INSPECTOR
MAYBRIDGE
MYSTERY

THE SUDDEN DEATH OF PROFESSOR PETER BRADSHAW AND HIS WIFE WAS RULED ACCIDENTAL....

But in light of the forensic pathologist's damning testimony in the Rapunzel murder cases—in which five prostitutes were strangled, long hair wrapped around their necks in a noose— Detective Chief Inspector Tom Maybridge decided to gently remind Bradshaw's teenage son that his father *did* have enemies....

Nobody had paid attention to the convicted killer's fervent tirades condemning Bradshaw's false testimony on the "Fifth Rapunzel." Perhaps it was time to listen.

"A cunningly twisted suspense mystery."
—*New York Times Book Review*

 WORLDWIDE LIBRARY®

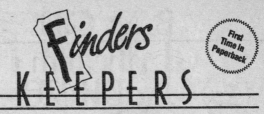

A Sheila Travis Mystery

MURDER

in the Charleston Manner

PATRICIA
HOUCK
SPRINKLE

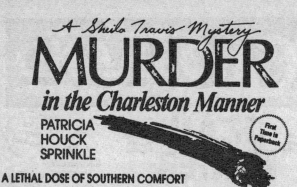

First Time in Paperback

A LETHAL DOSE OF SOUTHERN COMFORT

"Trouble follows that woman like fleas follow a dog," her father had always said about Aunt Mary. Sheila Travis ruefully agrees when she is dispatched by her colorful aunt to Charleston to "investigate" some mysterious accidents occurring at the historic home of Mary's childhood friends, Dolly and Marion.

Sheila's hostesses are a monument to Southern hospitality, and though a master at protocol, the former ambassador's wife feels boorish by comparison. But this isn't a social visit—Sheila has a job to do even if she's initially inclined to write the accidents off as coincidence. The first murder changes her mind....

"A plethora of likely suspects, all with motives, means and opportunity."
—*Booklist*

GHOSTLAND

JEAN HAGER

AN OKLAHOMA MYSTERY

First Time In Paperback

READING, WRITING AND MURDER

The Cherokee Heritage Festival is about to begin, and Buckskin, Oklahoma, is bustling—until the murder of Tamarah Birch, a third-grade girl from the tribal boarding school, dampens the festivities for the townspeople and especially for Police Chief Mitch Bushyhead.

Bushyhead has too few hard clues and too many suspects—a recently released mental patient, a school principal prone to fits of rage and an athletic coach who's departed previous jobs under suspicious circumstances.

"Hager's most engrossing effort to date."

—*Kirkus Reviews*
